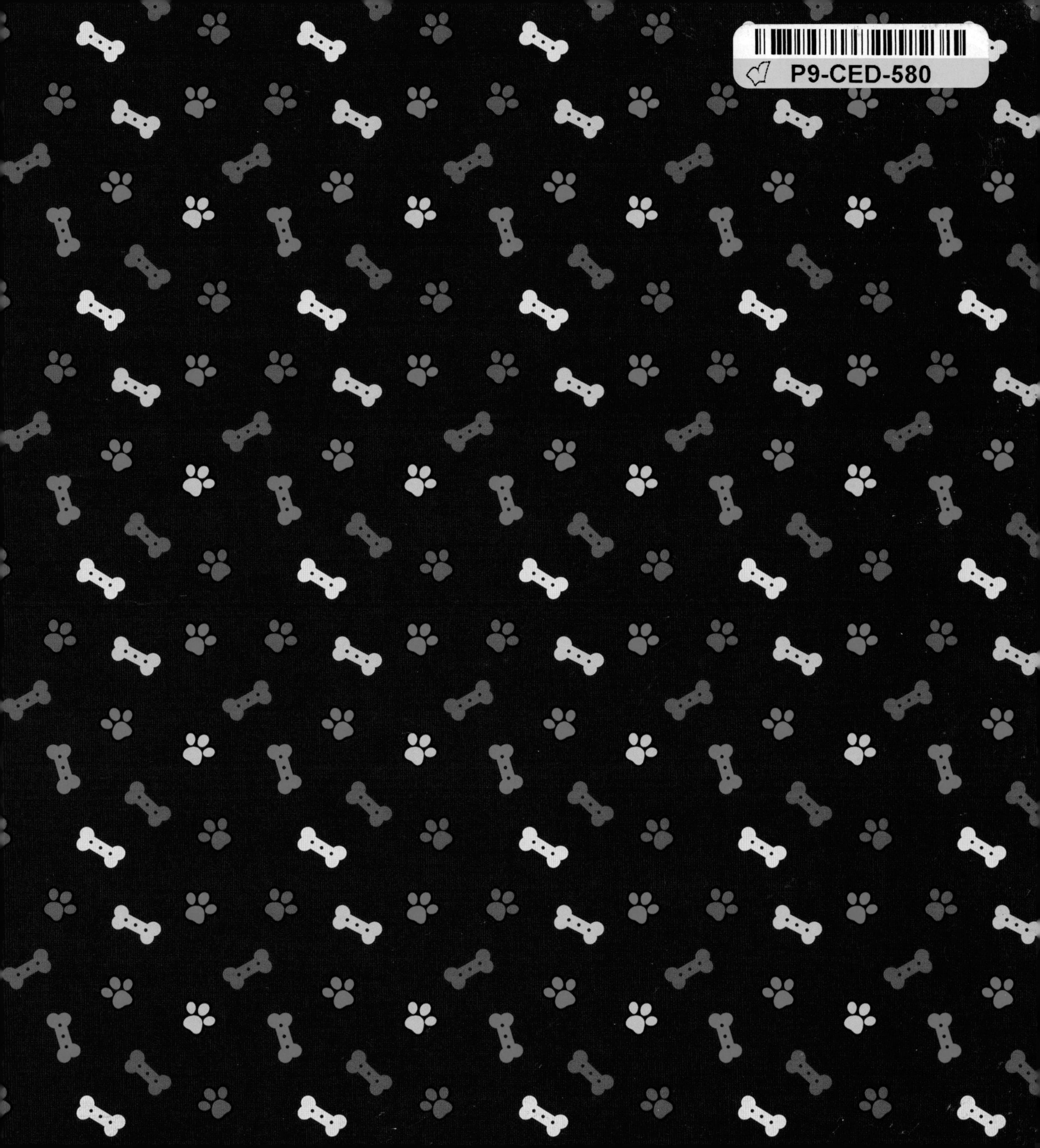

PAW PATROL™

Stories to Share

PAW PATROL

Stories to Share

Random House New York

Random House New York

 Published in the United States by Random House Children's Books, a division of Penguin Random House LLC, 1745 Broadway, New York, NY 10019, and in Canada by Penguin Random House Canada Limited, Toronto. The stories contained in this work were originally published separately in slightly different form by Random House Books for Young Readers as *High-Flying Skye* in 2016, by Tex Huntley, illustrated by MJ Illustrations; *Sea Patrol to the Rescue!* in 2018, by Geof Smith, illustrated by Nate Lovett; *Track That Monkey!* in 2019, by Casey Neumann, illustrated by MJ Illustrations; *Gold Rush Pups!* in 2017, by Tex Huntley, illustrated by MJ Illustrations; *Ready, Race, Rescue!* in 2019, by Hollis James, illustrated by MJ Illustrations; *King for a Day!* in 2016, by Mary Tillworth, illustrated by Mike Jackson; *Puppy Dance Party!* in 2019, by Hollis James, illustrated by Nate Lovett; *Ice Team* in 2015, by Geof Smith, illustrated by Mike Jackson; *Pup-Fu Power!* in 2016, by Tex Huntley, illustrated by Fabrizio Petrossi; *Pit Crew Pups* in 2015, by Kristen L. Depken, illustrated by Mike Jackson; *Chase's Space Case* in 2016, by Kristen L. Depken, illustrated by Mike Jackson; and *Pup, Pup, and Away!* in 2015, by Tex Huntley, illustrated by Harry Moore.

rhcbooks.com

ISBN 978-0-593-37536-5

MANUFACTURED IN CHINA

10 9 8 7 6 5 4 3 2 1

Stories to Share

High-Flying Skye

Late one afternoon, Skye was flying high over the Lookout. She was really excited because her hero, stunt pilot Ace Sorensen, was coming to the air show in Adventure Bay. Skye spun and spiraled and zipped and dipped.

"Trick flying is the best!" she exclaimed.

Down on the ground, Marshall wasn't sure he agreed. The only thing he liked to fly was his kite.

Suddenly, a big gust of wind caught Marshall's kite and blew him into the air. He got tangled in the kite's string and came crashing down—right on top of Rocky!

"Sorry," Marshall said with a grin. "I guess my landing was a little rocky."

Just then, Ryder got a call on his PupPad. It was Ace Sorensen, the stunt pilot! Her plane was having engine trouble, and she needed the PAW Patrol's help finding a place to land.

"We're on it!" Ryder declared. "No job is too big, no pup is too small!"

Ryder quickly called the pups to the Lookout and told them about Ace. He needed Skye's helicopter and her night-vision goggles.

"This pup's got to fly!" Skye yelped. She was eager to help her hero.

Ryder also needed Chase's spotlight and traffic cones to make a runway at Farmer Yumi's Farm.

"Chase is on the case!" barked the eager German shepherd.

Finally, Ryder asked Rocky to fix Ace's plane.

"Green means go!" Rocky cheered.

The sun was setting as Skye zoomed through the clouds in her helicopter. She scanned the darkening sky with her goggles and spotted something in the distance. "There she is now!"

Ace's damaged plane flew past a mountain and sputtered over the treetops. Black smoke poured out of the engine, making it even harder for Ace to see.

Skye pulled ahead of Ace's plane. "Follow me!" she called, and led the way to Farmer Yumi's Farm.

Meanwhile, at the farm, Ryder, Chase, and Rocky were preparing a runway so Ace could land. Chase set up his orange safety cones to mark off the landing strip.

"Great job!" Ryder said. As the sky continued to darken, he turned to Rocky and asked if he had any old flashlights in his truck.

"I've got a bunch," Rocky replied. He quickly collected the flashlights. Then he and Ryder taped them to the traffic cones.

When they were done, Ryder called Skye and told her to watch for the runway lights.

"Roger that!" said Skye.

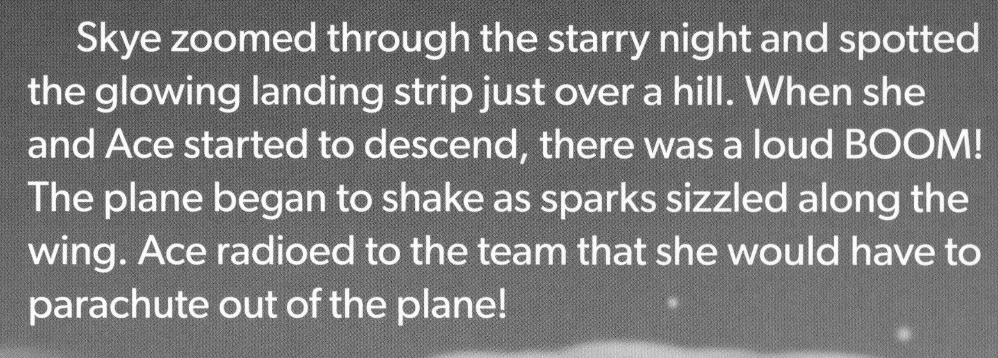

Skye zoomed through the starry night and spotted the glowing landing strip just over a hill. When she and Ace started to descend, there was a loud BOOM! The plane began to shake as sparks sizzled along the wing. Ace radioed to the team that she would have to parachute out of the plane!

Ryder didn't think parachuting in the dark was a good idea. He had another plan. "Ace, have you ever done the wing-walking stunt?" he asked.

"Ace is the greatest wing-walker in the whole world," Skye reported.

"Awesome!" Ryder exclaimed. He told Skye to lower her towline and safety harness.

Ace unbuckled her seat belt and carefully climbed onto the wing of her bouncing, shaking plane. Skye lowered her towline and harness and zoomed up close to Ace. The stunt pilot reached for the harness—but couldn't quite get it!

"I've got my parachute," Ace called. "I'm going to jump!"

"No!" Skye called back. "We can do this, Ace!"

Skye lowered her helicopter and flew in as close as she could. Ace tried again . . . and grabbed the harness! She snapped herself in and was carried through the air to Farmer Yumi's Farm.

As Skye approached the farm, Ace radioed Ryder and asked him to track someone named Amelia.

"Sure," Ryder said. "But who's Amelia?"

"My plane," Ace replied. "Every great pilot names her plane."

Ryder tracked the plane on his PupPad and saw that it was heading for a water landing in the bay!

"Let's find the plane and get it onto the beach before it sinks!" said Ryder.

Ryder and Chase raced to the bay, and Skye gently set Ace down at the farm. The stunt pilot unfastened the harness and waved up to the helicopter. "Thanks, Skye!" she called.

"No problem, Ace!" the pilot pup called back. Then she whispered excitedly to herself, "I can't believe I saved my hero!"

Splash! Amelia sputtered, then glided to a stop in the bay. Ryder sped out to the plane on his Jet Ski and hooked a cable to it. When Ryder gave the command, Chase turned on his winch and pulled *Amelia* to shore.

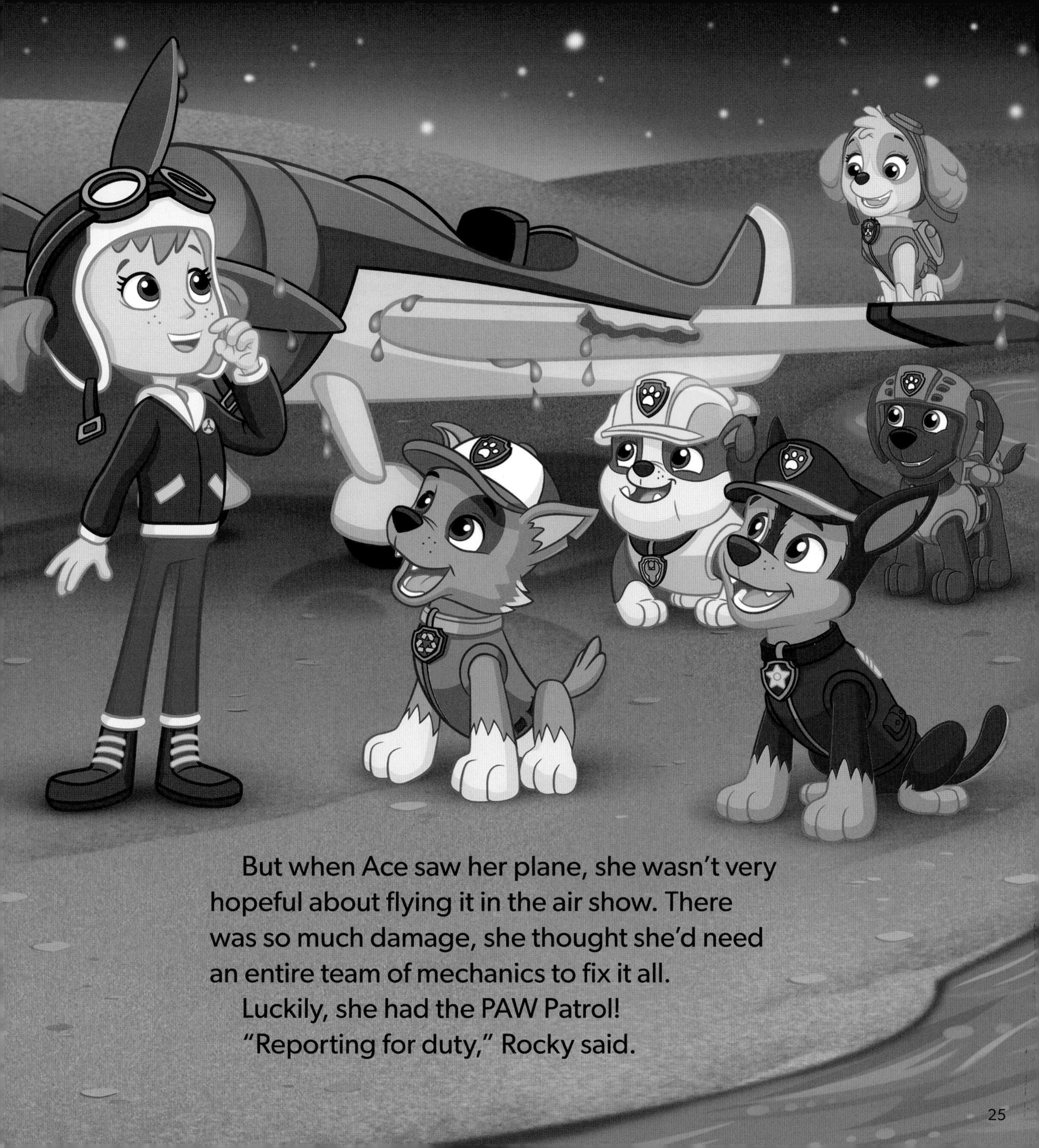

But when Ace saw her plane, she wasn't very hopeful about flying it in the air show. There was so much damage, she thought she'd need an entire team of mechanics to fix it all.

Luckily, she had the PAW Patrol!

"Reporting for duty," Rocky said.

By the glow of Chase's spotlight, Rocky riveted a patch onto Amelia's wing. At the same time, Ryder fixed the cockpit, while Ace adjusted the engine. In no time, Skye started up the plane. The propeller began to spin, and the engine roared. The plane was as good as new!

"I can't wait for the air show tomorrow," Skye said.

Ace hopped onto one of the wings. "How would you like to see my wing-walk-and-roll trick up close and personal?"

Skye thought that sounded great!

The next day was sunny and warm, and the PAW Patrol watched the air show from Adventure Bay's beach. They cheered and waved as *Amelia* flew into view. Ace climbed out of the cockpit and stood on a wing. Then the plane tilted slightly, and they saw Skye smiling behind the controls.

Suddenly, Ace jumped into the air, and Skye made the plane twirl around. When the plane was level again, Ace landed back on the wing. Ryder and the pups couldn't believe their eyes. The wing-walk-and-roll trick was the most amazing stunt they'd ever seen!

"Wow!" Rocky gasped, watching Skye zoom through the clouds. "She's so good!"

"You're all good pups," Ryder said.

The pups cheered and barked for each other as Skye and Ace zipped overhead.

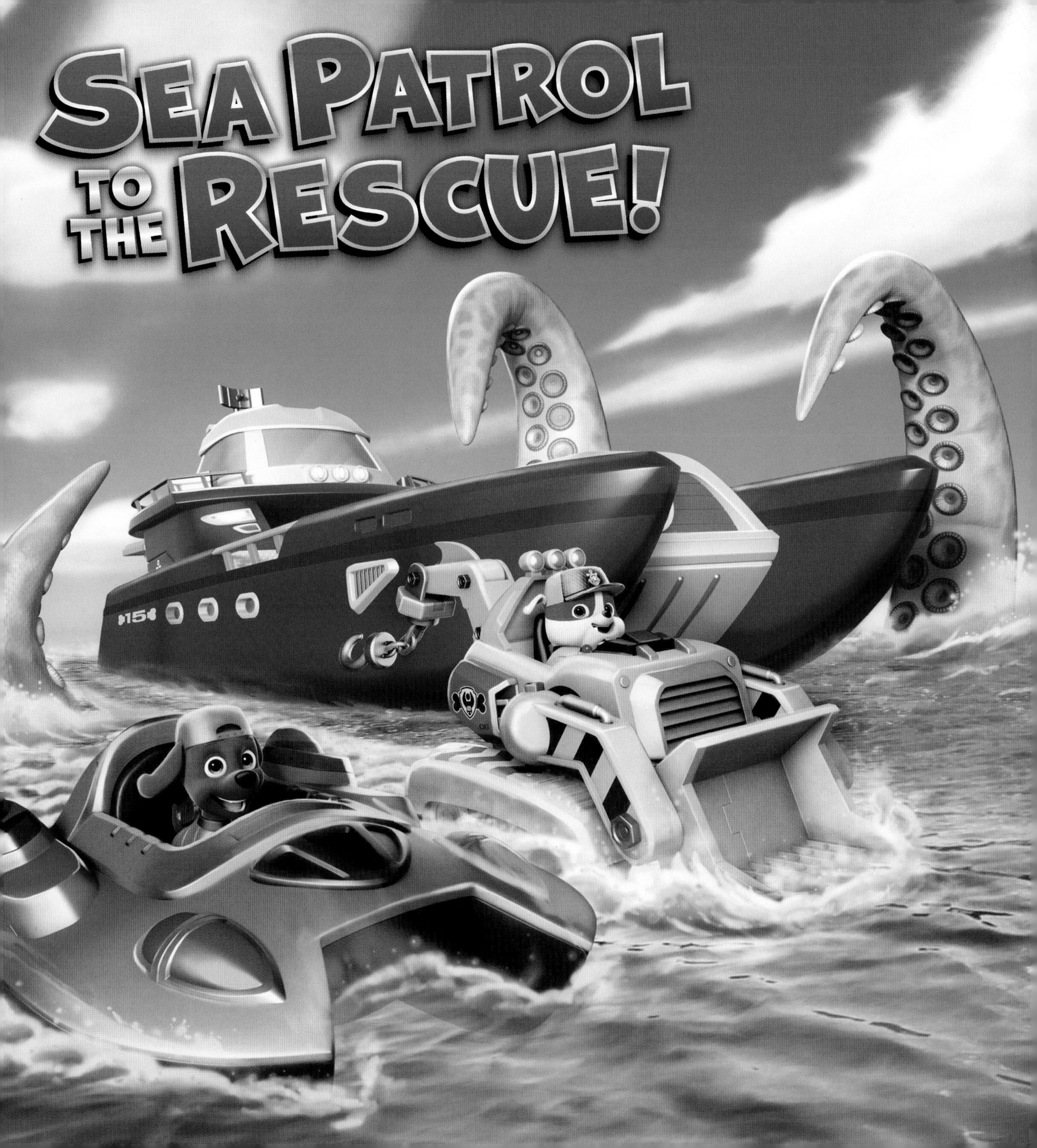
SEA PATROL
TO THE RESCUE!

One sunny morning, the PAW Patrol were at their new Beach Tower headquarters. Mayor Goodway had asked the pups to be Adventure Beach's new lifeguard rescue team. She wanted them on duty during her luau that afternoon.

"We'll be the Sea Patrol," Ryder announced. "But before you can save anyone, you'll have to earn your lifeguard badges."

"Ready, set, get wet!" barked Zuma.

For the lifeguard test, the pups didn't rescue a person. They took turns swimming through a course of floating buoys and rescuing a pineapple named Mr. Prickly! One by one, each pup earned a badge . . . until it was Rocky's turn.

"That's okay," he said. "I don't like getting wet."

"You can't be a lifeguard without getting wet," Skye said.

"Hmmm," Rocky said to himself. "We'll see about that!"

Instead of swimming, Rocky jumped from buoy to buoy, then threw a life ring around Mr. Prickly. He pulled the pineapple in and hopped back to shore without getting wet!

"Cool rescue technique," Ryder said. "But if you want to earn your lifeguard badge, you have to swim."

Rocky was happy to be a land guard.

"I know you can do this," said Ryder. "If you don't feel up to it now, you can try again later."

Meanwhile, Cap'n Turbot was out at sea feeding Wally the Walrus. "Here's some more juicy jellyfish jerky," he said. He didn't realize that a baby octopus was stuck to the side of his chum bucket.

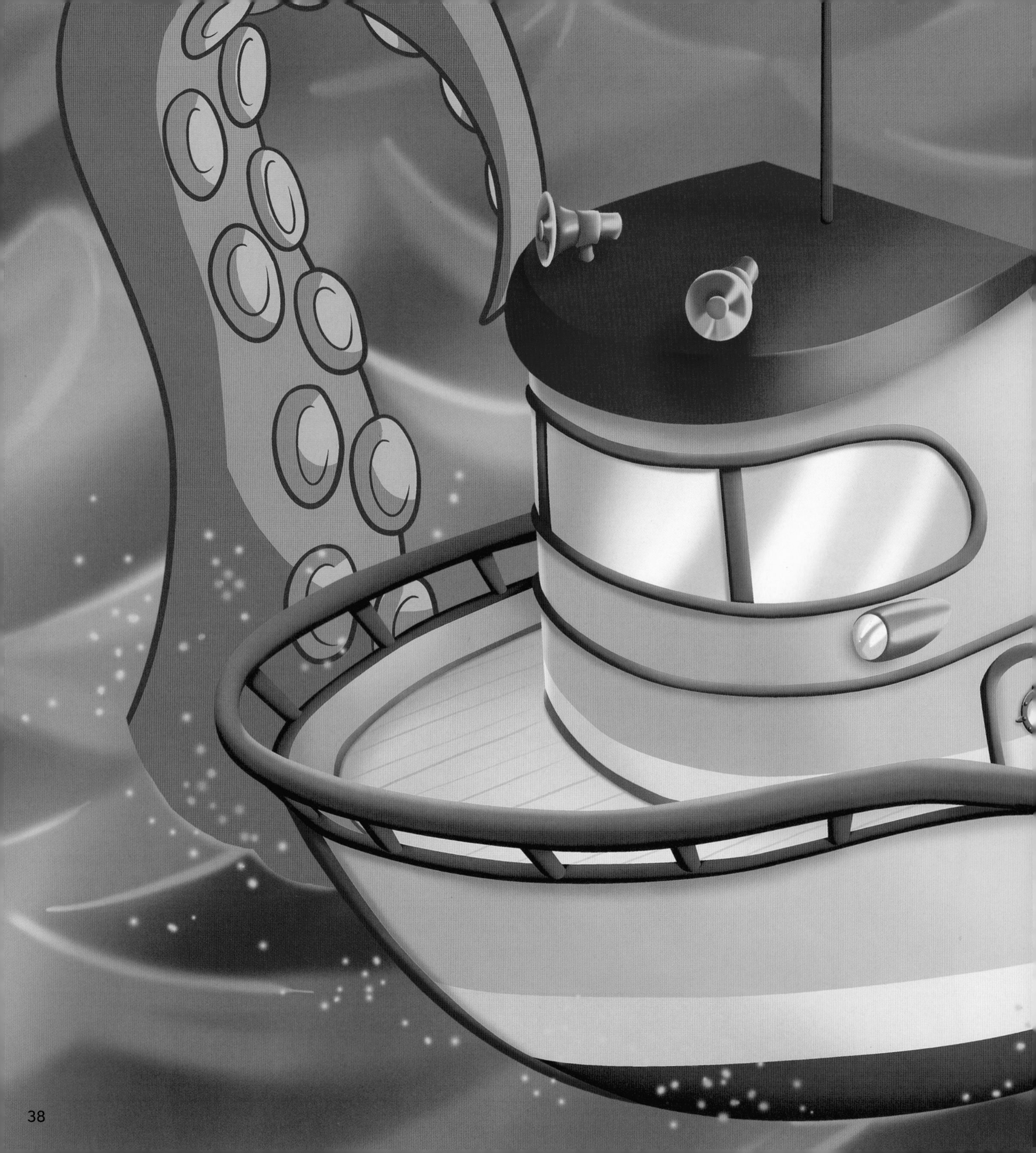

Suddenly, the water started churning, and Cap'n Turbot's boat, the *Flounder,* began to rock. Giant tentacles reached out of the waves and wrapped around the boat.

"Great gushing geysers—I need the PAW Patrol!" Cap'n Turbot exclaimed, and he called Ryder.

Ryder told the pups about Cap'n Turbot's boat. "The Sea Patrol is on a roll!"

"Um, Ryder, how are we going to get out to the *Flounder*?" Rubble asked.

Ryder pushed a button on his PupPad.

The Beach Tower shook as a huge ship called the *Sea Patroller* detached from it. Robo Dog was at the controls, and he loaded Zuma's and Rubble's special sea vehicles onto it.

Ryder, Rubble, Zuma, and Marshall hopped aboard, and the *Sea Patroller* sped to the rescue.

The *Sea Patroller* reached the troubled *Flounder.* Zuma and Rubble hit the waves in their new sea vehicles.

Zuma tried to pull the tentacles off Cap'n Turbot's boat with his vehicle's mechanical arms, but the sea monster was too strong.

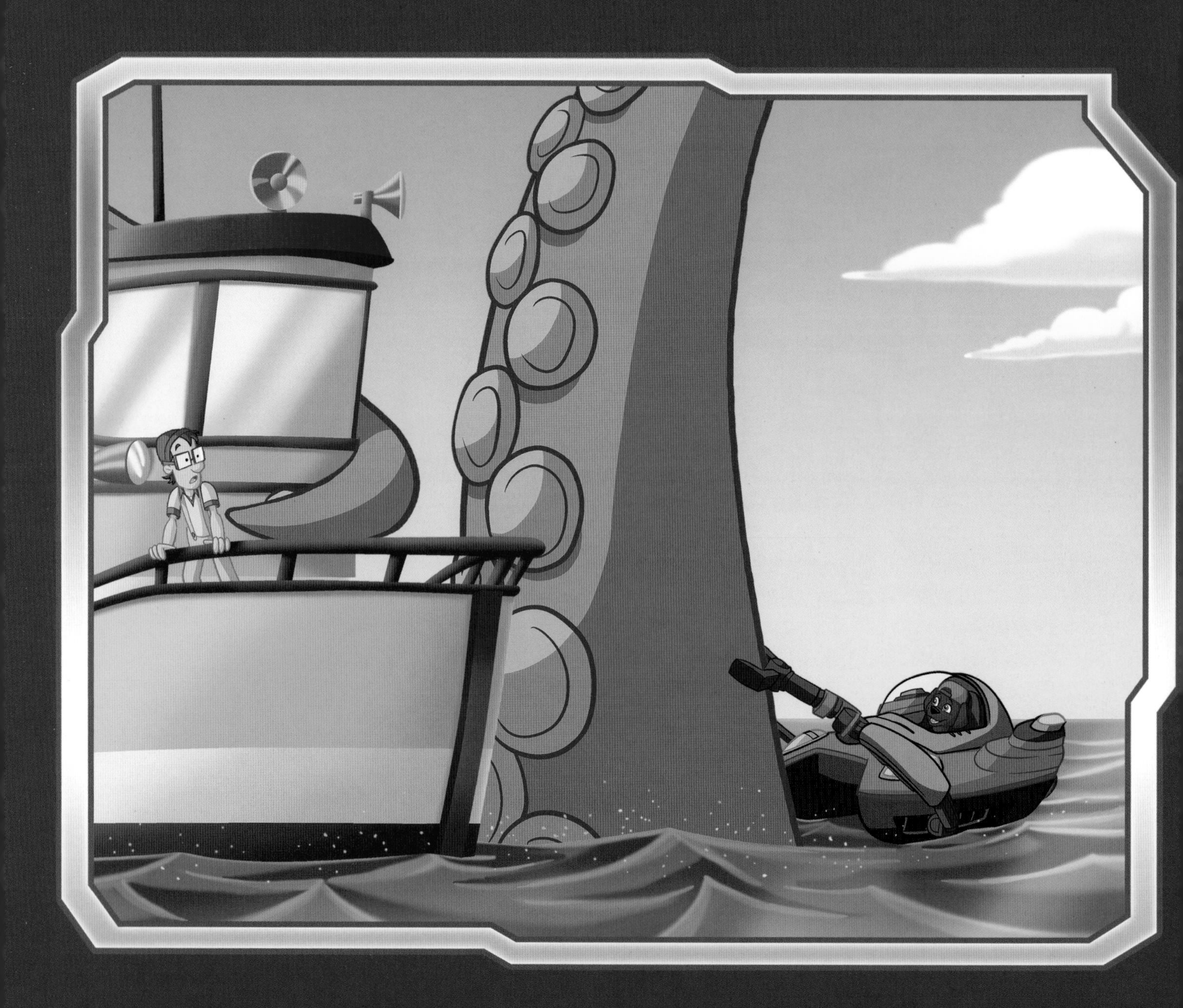

Ryder had an idea. He told Robo Dog to sound the *Sea Patroller*'s horn.

BWAAAAAAAA!

The startled sea monster released the *Flounder* and slid back below the ocean's surface.

"Hooray!" everyone cheered.

But just then, the *Flounder* started to sink—and Cap'n Turbot was still on it!

Rubble used his crane to pluck Cap'n Turbot off the deck—just as the boat slipped under the waves.

"The pups and I will do everything we can to raise the *Flounder*," Ryder promised.

As Rubble headed back to land, no one noticed the little stowaway stuck to Cap'n Turbot's life ring.

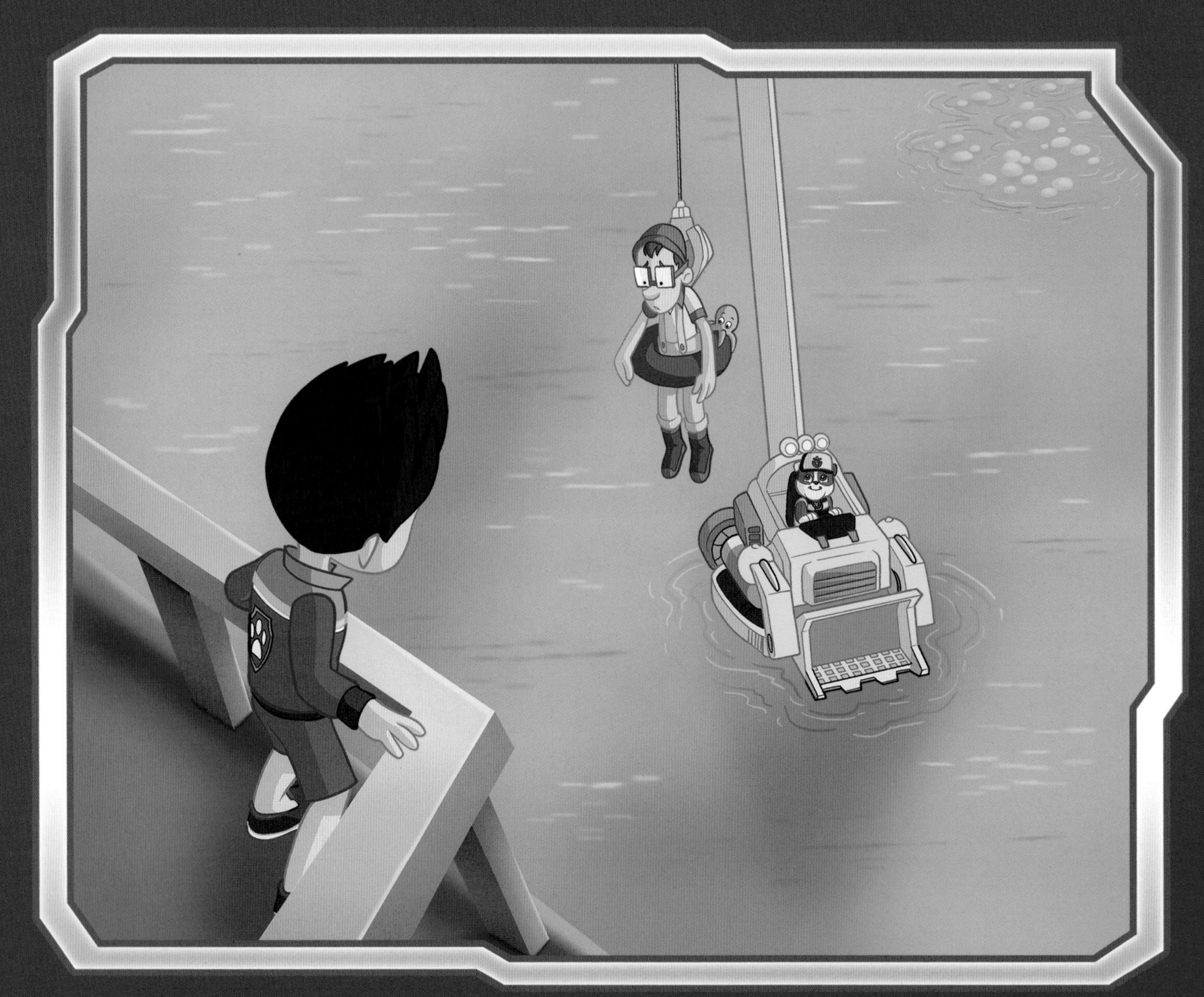

Marshall put on his scuba gear, dove into the water, and went to work. He found the sunken *Flounder* and started pumping it full of air from his tanks. The boat floated up toward the surface.

As Marshall watched the boat rise, something shiny caught his eye. Was it undersea treasure?

He picked it up with his mechanical claw and shook it. "It's a baby rattle!" he exclaimed.

Meanwhile, Cap'n Turbot was back on Adventure Beach trying to cheer himself up at Mayor Goodway's luau. But while he looked for something to eat, the baby octopus jumped off him and landed on Mayor Humdinger's head!

"Help!" the mayor shouted. "Get it off!"

Just then, the sea monster rose out of the waves! Skye took to the air with her parasail to distract it while Rubble built a sand wall to protect the beachgoers.

When Ryder arrived, he saw that the sea monster was actually an octopus—and it was squinting. "It's looking for something, but it can't see very well."

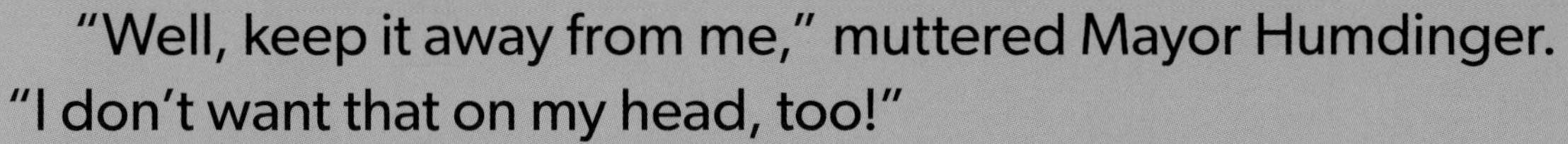

"Well, keep it away from me," muttered Mayor Humdinger. "I don't want that on my head, too!"

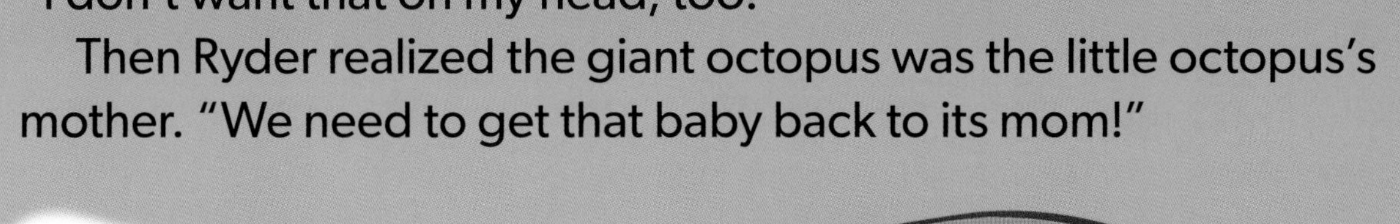

Then Ryder realized the giant octopus was the little octopus's mother. "We need to get that baby back to its mom!"

But first they had to get the baby off Mayor Humdinger's head. Marshall remembered the rattle he'd found and started shaking it.

The baby octopus reached for the toy . . . but because Mayor Humdinger couldn't see, he accidentally knocked the rattle into the ocean!

Someone had to get that rattle!

"I can find it with my metal detector," said Rocky.

"Are you sure, Rocky?" Ryder asked. "You'll have to swim and get wet."

"If getting wet will help the baby octopus get back to its mom, I can do it!" Rocky declared. He extended his metal detector, bravely dove into the water, and found the rattle!

Shaking the toy, Zuma boarded the *Sea Patroller* with Ryder and headed away from the beach. The little octopus followed the rattling noise . . . and the mother followed her baby. Out in the deep water, the mother and baby found each other and hugged.

Ryder quickly made eyeglasses out of two punch bowls from the luau. Now the mother could always find her baby.

The Sea Patrol had worked together and saved the day!

Back on the beach, everyone cheered for the pups—and for Cap'n Turbot's newly repaired *Flounder.*

"Thank you, PAW Patrol," said Mayor Goodway. "You saved the beach *and* the party!"

"I think Rocky deserves the biggest thank-you," said Ryder. "He got wet to save the day and earned this." Ryder pinned a lifeguard badge to Rocky's vest. All the pups howled and hoorayed for their brave friend!

TRACK THAT MONKEY!

One day, the PAW Patrol were in the jungle helping their friends Carlos and Tracker give the monkeys their yearly checkups. Tracker used his magnifying glass to examine Mandy the monkey.

"I'm ready to take Mandy's X-ray!" said Marshall.

Mandy put her face behind Marshall's scanner. The image of her bones surprised the other monkeys, and they started running in circles.

"Uh-oh! How do we calm them down?" asked Rocky.

"Scratch their backs!" said Carlos. "Monkeys love that!"

Rocky extended the claw from his Pup Pack and went to work scratching backs. The monkeys quickly relaxed.

"Looks like you've made some new friends, Rocky!" Marshall yelped.

Just then, a giant monkey named Big Hairy peeked around the rock he was hiding behind and saw Rocky's back scratcher. He really wanted to have his back scratched!

Chase and Zuma arrived, back from searching the jungle.

"We looked all over, but we didn't find any more monkeys who need a checkup," said Chase.

Carlos decided it was time to close the monkey checkup center. He thanked the PAW Patrol for their help.

Marshall invited Tracker to come back with the pups for a visit.

The pups happily scampered into the PAW Patroller as Carlos and the monkeys waved goodbye.

The PAW Patroller rumbled along the jungle road. Suddenly, big bunches of bananas landed on the roof.

"¿Escucharon?" Tracker asked. "Did anyone else hear that?"

Ryder and the pups didn't see anything outside.

"Probably just some bumps in the road," Ryder suggested. They didn't realize that Big Hairy was riding on the roof of their vehicle!

As the PAW Patroller rolled into town, Big Hairy saw the giant cup on top of Mr. Porter's lemonade stand. He leaped from the vehicle onto the stand's roof. He rubbed his back against the huge cup—and it broke loose and crashed to the ground!

Next, Big Hairy ran to the statue of Chickaletta in front of city hall and rubbed his back against it. The statue fell over with a thud!

The giant monkey quickly ran off to find something else to scratch his back on.

Mayor Goodway discovered the statue of Chickaletta lying on the sidewalk.

"How did this happen?" she cried. Then she heard the sound of bells ringing and looked up. She couldn't believe her eyes—a giant monkey was shaking the bell tower on top of city hall!

Mayor Goodway immediately called the PAW Patrol.

Ryder gathered the pups at the Lookout and told them about Big Hairy.

"We'd better get him home before he causes any more monkey trouble!" he said.

For this mission, Ryder needed Rocky's big claw and catapult. He also needed Tracker's jeep and his super hearing.

"Green means go!" shouted Rocky.

"I'm all ears!" Tracker exclaimed. *"¡Todos oídos!"*

"The PAW Patrol is on the roll!" Ryder said. He and the two pups rushed to their vehicles.

The team found Big Hairy outside Mr. Porter's market. Rocky used his catapult to launch bananas at the monkey. Tracker tried to lure him away by pulling the banana-filled wagon with his cables.

The giant monkey wasn't interested.

"Why isn't he going after the bananas?" Rocky asked.

That was when Ryder noticed that Big Hairy was scratching his fur and pointing at Rocky's claw.

"He wants his back scratched with the best back scratcher ever, like the other monkeys did!" said Ryder.

Just then, Big Hairy grabbed Rocky and took off!

"After that giant monkey!" shouted Ryder.

Ryder called the rest of the PAW Patrol together. They chased Big Hairy and surrounded him on a bridge.

"Big Hairy, please let Rocky go!" begged Ryder.

But Big Hairy didn't want to. He turned and leaped off the bridge!

Big Hairy landed safely on the deck of Cap'n Turbot's boat, the *Flounder.*

"Sizzling sea serpents—I've never seen such a super-sized simian!" Cap'n Turbot exclaimed. "I need to shoot a series of snaps!"

He reached for his camera, but before he could get a shot, Big Hairy was gone!

Big Hairy made his way to the Lookout and climbed to the top of the tower.

Chase used his megaphone to check on Rocky.

"How are you doing up there, Rocky?" he called.

"I'm okay," Rocky replied. "But I'm getting tired of scratching!"

After a moment, Ryder had an idea!

Skye swooped in and nudged Big Hairy away from the edge of the roof. Then Zuma moved the periscope up and down from the control room to scratch Big Hairy's back.

He was so relaxed, he let go of Rocky.

Tracker used his cables as a zip line to bring Rocky down safely.
"Great work, Tracker!" said Ryder.

Skye dangled a bunch of bananas just out of Big Hairy's reach, then slowly lowered them to the roof. The giant monkey climbed down the Lookout and followed Skye to the PAW Patroller.

Everything was back to normal . . . except Big Hairy's back was still itchy!

Rocky ran over to Big Hairy and gave him a giant back scratcher.

"I made you something to remember me by!" Rocky exclaimed.

Big Hairy was thrilled. He grabbed his new back scratcher and hopped onto the roof of the PAW Patroller. He was ready to head back to the jungle!

Ryder asked Robo Dog to take Big Hairy home, and soon the PAW Patroller began to roll away. Everyone said goodbye to the big monkey.

"And remember," Ryder called, "whenever you have an itch, just *ooka-ooka* for help!"

The pups laughed and cheered.

GOLD RUSH PUPS!

One sunny day, Rubble was digging for gold with Chickaletta, Mayor Goodway, and her uncle Otis. Unfortunately, Uncle Otis's prospecting tools were really old. His shovel broke, and the bottom fell out of his gold-straining pan.

Uncle Otis needed help, and Rubble and the mayor knew just who to call—the PAW Patrol!

Ryder, Chase, and Rocky rode to the rescue. Rocky had the perfect recycled tools: a used shovel for Uncle Otis and some old strainers so everyone could pan for gold. They all went to work beside the river.

Suddenly, Chickaletta found a shiny rock. It was gold! Chase and Ryder found some, too. Soon they had a big pile of glittering gold.

Since Chickaletta had found the first gold nugget, Mayor Goodway wanted to build a big golden statue of her feathery friend.

"Good idea!" said Ryder. "C'mon, pups—the more gold we find, the bigger the statue!"

Not far away, Mayor Humdinger from Foggy Bottom was watching the pups and their friends. "That gold is mine, because . . . um . . . I want it!"

He planned to make a golden statue of himself, so he radioed his Kitten Catastrophe Crew. "Kittens, it's catastrophe time!"

Mayor Humdinger joined Ryder and the pup prospectors. When no one was looking, the mean mayor snuck something into his strainer.

"What's this?" he said. "A diamond!"

Everyone was amazed by the mayor's discovery.

While the others studied the diamond, the Kitten Catastrophe Crew loaded the gold onto a little truck.

Uncle Otis peered closely at the mayor's find. "This is no diamond," he said. "It's just rock candy!" The friends turned around just in time to see Mayor Humdinger getting away with the gold!

The PAW Patrol was on the roll.

"Chase, we need your drone!" Ryder exclaimed.

A drone flew out of Chase's truck. It zoomed into the air and tracked Mayor Humdinger and his kittens.

The mayor and his crew raced to their mountain hideout.

"Home, sweet home, kitties," he announced. "Don't forget the gold!"

They all ran into their secret cave, but no one brought the gold inside.

Chase's drone led Ryder and the pups right to Mayor Humdinger's hideout—and the stolen gold!

"Rocky, unhook the wagon," Ryder said.

"You got it!" exclaimed Rocky.

Ryder had a plan to stop the sneaky kittens from chasing after the gold. "Let it go, Rubble!" he shouted.

Rubble pushed a big boulder in front of the hideout's entrance, temporarily trapping Mayor Humdinger and the Kitten Catastrophe Crew.

"Nooo!" Mayor Humdinger cried as Ryder and the pups rode away with the gold. "I deserve to be a statue!"

A few days later in Adventure Bay, Mayor Goodway unveiled a giant golden statue of Chickaletta. Ryder, Uncle Otis, and all the pups cheered when the little chicken perched on top.

"She loves it!" Mayor Goodway exclaimed, and everyone cheered for Chickaletta.

03
READY, RACE, RESCUE!

It was the day of the Adventure Bay 500, a very important car race. All the best racers were there: Riff Rockinbock, Lionel Lightspeed, Willy Widewheels Jr., and the mighty Whoosh! The PAW Patrol was excited to be the pit crew.

"Marshall, you must be the Whoosh's biggest fan-pup ever," said Skye.

"I am," said Marshall. "I've seen every one of his races!"

Just then, the Cheetah screeched up to the starting line. She was Mayor Humdinger's niece and a very sneaky racer.

"Eat my dust, pups!" she said when the qualifying race began.

"And they're off—except for the Whoosh!" said Ron Rapidfire, the announcer. "He seems to be stuck at the starting line."

Mayor Humdinger had ordered his Kitten Catastrophe Crew to glue the Whoosh's tires to the track!

"I'm ready to do a *ruff-ruff* repair!" said Marshall, who had his hydroblaster.

"I've got lots more dirty tricks," said the Cheetah, pushing a button in her car. A spear came out of her wheel and punctured Lionel Lightspeed's tire!

“Don’t worry, Lionel,” said Ryder. “The pit-crew pups will get you back in the race!”

The PAW Patrol raced to the rescue in their brand-new Mobile Pit Stop.

Riff's speakers were blasting loud music as he caught up to the Cheetah.

"I've got a new song for you," said the Cheetah. "It's called 'The Foggy Bottom Blues.'"

She pushed a button, and a blue fog immediately sprayed from her car. Both Willy and Riff crashed!

The Mobile Pit Crew was quickly on the scene.

"Wow, the pit-crew pups have had their paws full today!" declared Ron Rapidfire.

Cheetah pushed another button, and another dirty trick took the Whoosh out of the race!

"Whoosh, are you okay?" asked Marshall.

"I must have banged my arm," said the Whoosh. "I can't drive like this—but *you* can drive, Marshall."

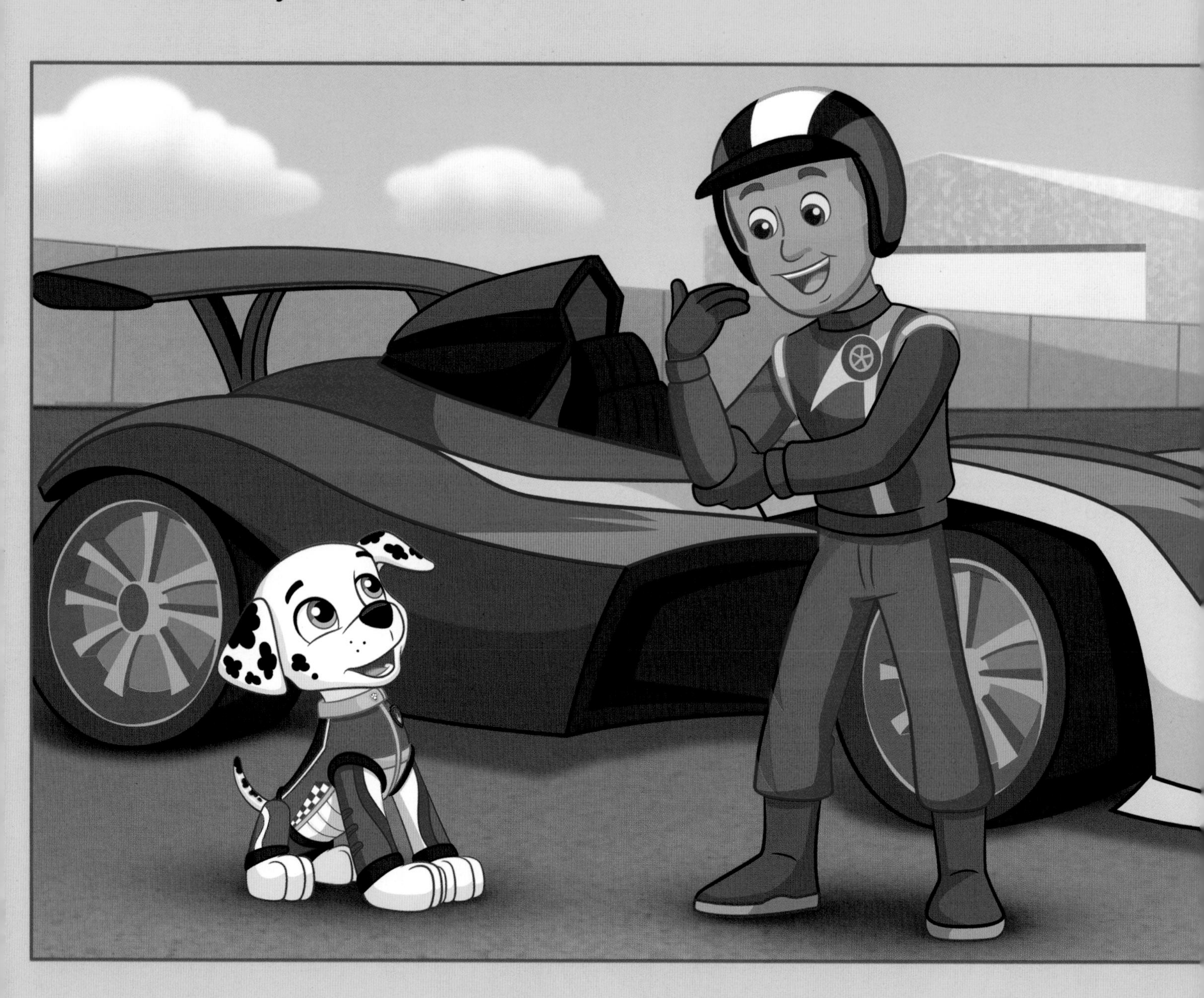

Marshall couldn't say no to his favorite driver, so he took the Whoosh's place in the next race. He zoomed along the track, screeching around the turns.

"Marshall has taken the lead as they head for the finish line!" announced Ron Rapidfire.

"That's pup's finished, all right," said the Cheetah. "Now to slingshot to victory. See ya!"

With that, the Cheetah fired a rope at Marshall's car, which pulled him back while she zoomed ahead of him. Marshall's car went spinning!

"And the winner of the Adventure Bay 500 is . . . the Cheetah!" said Ron.
There was one more race left—the Road Rally Championship.

The Whoosh's arm wouldn't be better in time for the championship, so he trained Marshall to take his place. He taught the pup how to drift, slide, and glide.

"I've got a very serious and important racing tip for you," said the Whoosh. "Smile, buddy! Racing is fun."

"I can definitely do that!" said Marshall.

In the Cheetah's hideout, the Humdingers were making plans.

"The Whoosh is training that pup to race against you," said Mayor Humdinger.

The Cheetah thought for a moment. "We need to upgrade my race car . . . by taking the best parts from everyone else's!"

Mayor Humdinger used his blimp to steal the other drivers' cars.

He even snatched up the Whoosh so he couldn't coach Marshall!

"This rescue has a need for speed!" Ryder declared.

He used the Mobile Pit Stop to jazz up all the pups' rescue vehicles. Engines revved and roared as the PAW Patrol raced to the rescue!

Back at the track, it was time for the championship race. The Cheetah rolled up in her racer, which had been turbocharged with all the best parts from the stolen cars.

"There's no one to challenge the Cheetah!" exclaimed Mayor Goodway.

"I guess that means I win," said the Cheetah.

Just then, Marshall rolled up in his super-rescue car.

"I'm racing for Team Whoosh!" he declared. But then he radioed Ryder. "Have you rescued the Whoosh yet? I could really use his coaching about now."

"We're still after him, Marshall," Ryder replied. "Hang in there!"

"Ready, set, race!" said Mayor Goodway, and the cars sped off!

Meanwhile, the rest of the pups worked together to save the Whoosh. Skye caught Mayor Humdinger's blimp in her turbojet.

Rocky built a ramp . . .

. . . which Chase used to launch himself midair to free the Whoosh.

The Whoosh fell into the bay, where Zuma picked him up!

The race went on. The Cheetah tried her slingshot move again. Marshall began to spin out of control, just like before. But then he remembered what the Whoosh had taught him. He stayed calm and steered through the spin.

"Way to go, Marshall!" said a familiar voice through Marshall's Pup Tag.

"Whoosh!" exclaimed Marshall. "You're back!"

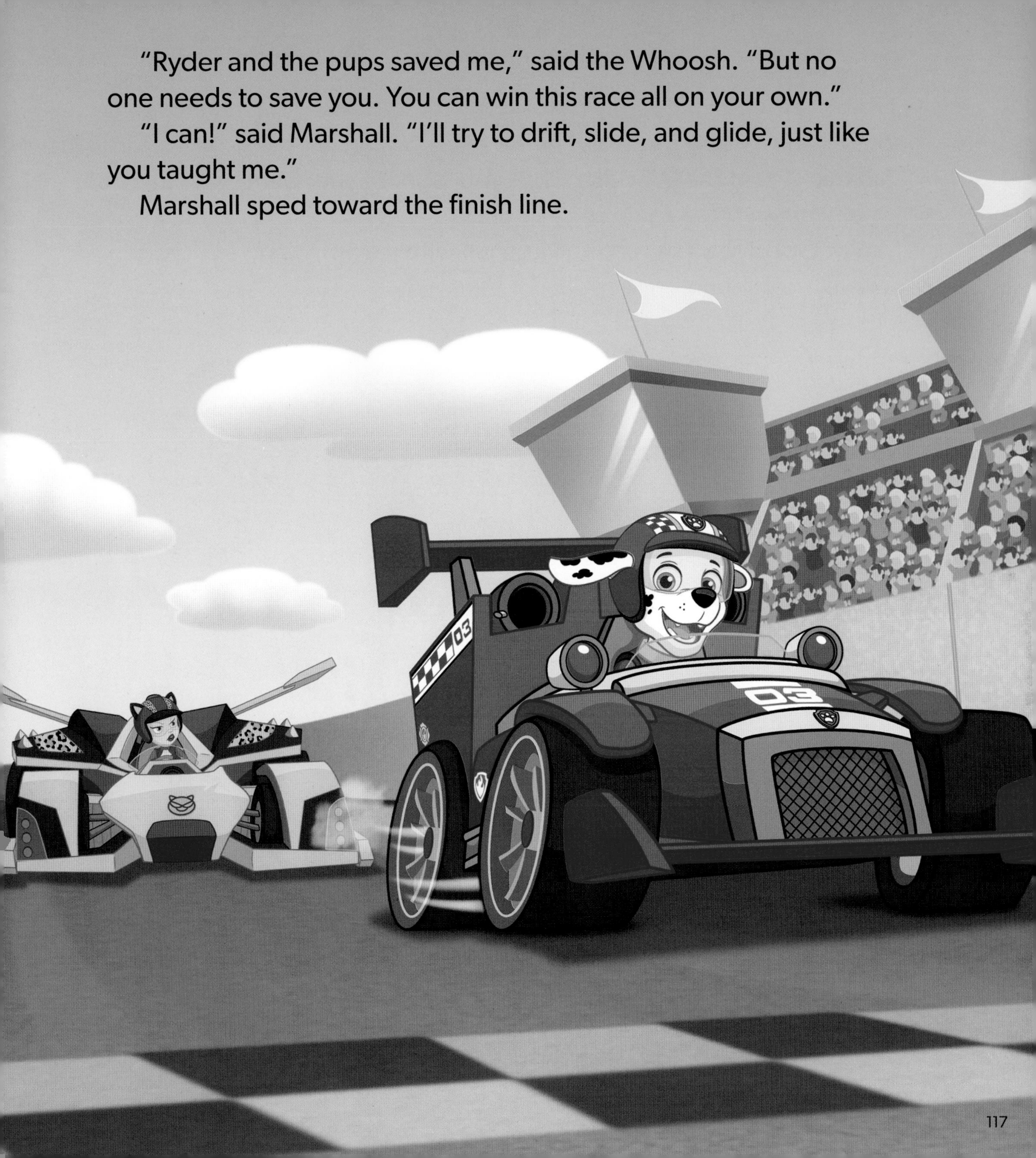

"Ryder and the pups saved me," said the Whoosh. "But no one needs to save you. You can win this race all on your own."

"I can!" said Marshall. "I'll try to drift, slide, and glide, just like you taught me."

Marshall sped toward the finish line.

He won the race!

"This championship really belongs to the Whoosh," Marshall declared. "I couldn't have won it without him."

"Thanks," said the Whoosh, "but you won on your own, with the true heart of a racer!"

Mayor Goodway presented Marshall with a trophy, and everyone cheered!

KING for a DAY!

"Fear not, fair princess!" Marshall cried. "The Pups of the Round Table will save thee!"

The pups were practicing their play about knights. Chase was King Arthur, and the other pups were his brave knights.

"Our play will be *knight*-tastic!" Marshall declared.

In Adventure Bay's town square, Cap'n Turbot was building the set for the play. The set looked like a castle!

"Castle construction is close to completion!" Cap'n Turbot announced. "Just one last nail . . ."

But when he swung his hammer, he missed! Instead of hitting the nail, he hit the castle wall, and . . .

. . . the set collapsed!

A big piece of the castle fell right on top of Cap'n Turbot.

"I'm stuck!" he cried. He reached for his phone and called the PAW Patrol for help.

"Don't worry, Cap'n Turbot," Ryder said. "No job is too big, no pup is too small!"

The PAW Patrol raced to the town square.

"How are you, Cap'n Turbot?" Marshall asked.

"Super! But stuck," he said. "And my arm smarts a smidge."

"We'll have you out in no time!" Ryder promised. "Rubble, use your claw hook to lift the wall."

"On the double!" Rubble said.

Rubble backed his truck up to the wall and lifted it away from Cap'n Turbot. But there was still another piece of scenery trapping him.

Chase used the winch on his vehicle to pull the doorway off Cap'n Turbot. He was free!

"Thanks, PAW Patrol!" Cap'n Turbot said as he stood and brushed himself off.

"Okay, Cap'n Turbot!" Marshall said. "I need to do a medical exam. X-ray machine!"

The machine popped out of Marshall's pack. He used it to scan Cap'n Turbot's bones.

"Hmm," Marshall said. "Looks like it's only a sprain. I'll wrap it up."

A bandage popped out of Marshall's pack. He wrapped the bandage around Cap'n Turbot's wrist.

Cap'n Turbot needed to rest his arm, so it was up to the PAW Patrol to finish building the castle for their play.

"Okay, my Pups of the Round Table!" Chase commanded through his megaphone. "Moveth!"

Skye used her helicopter and a towing cable to fly a wall to the set. She placed it in the middle of the stage.

Rocky popped a tool arm out of his pack. *ZZRRRZZZ!* He used the power screwdriver to spin screws through a hinge and into the wooden door. He tested the door to make sure it could easily open and close.

"This castle door is ready!" he announced.

Marshall held a paintbrush in his mouth and dipped it into a can of purple paint. He carefully spread the paint on the wall.

Ryder worked on the other side of the doorway. Together, they finished painting the castle in a flash!

Soon the castle was ready! The pups felt so proud, they all howled and barked.

Except Chase. He didn't bark—he coughed!

Marshall took his temperature. "Uh-oh. You've got a fever! You need lots of rest and liquids."

But who would play King Arthur in the play?

Marshall! He knew all the lines! And the crown fit him.

It was time to start the entertainment, and the last of the audience arrived just before the play began. Cali the kitten was a princess stuck high in a tower. The pup who pulled the bone from the stone would become king and save the princess.

"Behold! The bone!" Rubble said.

"Mmm," Rocky said, licking his lips. "It looks-eth delicious!"

Marshall entered. "Fear not, fair princess!"

He jumped over the bone and took it in his teeth. Then he struggled to pull it out of the stone.

WHOOOP! When the bone came free, it flew out of Marshall's mouth and hit the tower! The tower toppled over, and Cali fell!

The audience gasped!

Thankfully, Marshall caught Cali—and he remembered to say his line. "You are free, fair princess!"

The audience cheered. Marshall was doing an excellent job!

Lady Skye popped the wings out of her pack and flew over Marshall. "Heads up!" she said as she dropped a golden crown right onto his head.

It was a perfect fit!

"All hail King Arthur!" the pups cried, kneeling in front of Marshall.

The curtain closed. When it opened again, the pups took a bow. The audience cheered again!

"Great job, all of you!" Ryder said. "You're such good pups!"

The king had saved the day.

And Marshall had saved the play!

PUPPY
DANCE
PARTY!

Mayor Goodway was super excited—it was Chicken Day! Outside city hall, she was busy getting ready for a big party to celebrate her pet chicken, Chickaletta. The mayor had decorated the park with bales of hay and balloons. She had even put on a chicken costume!

Just then, Mayor Goodway saw Mr. Porter pushing his snack cart and his popcorn popper. Alex rolled along next to him on his skateboard.

"Oh, Mr. Porter, I'm so relieved to see you," said Mayor Goodway. "Did you make these special Chicken Day treats?"

"Yes," said Mr. Porter. "Just like you asked. I've got corncobs, corn muffins, corn dogs on a stick . . ."

"Popcorn?" asked Mayor Goodway.

"Right here!" said Mr. Porter.

But when he turned around, he saw that his popcorn popper was gone!

"Uh . . . uh . . . where did it go?" said Mr. Porter. "I'll be back in a jiffy."

He ran off to look for his missing popper.

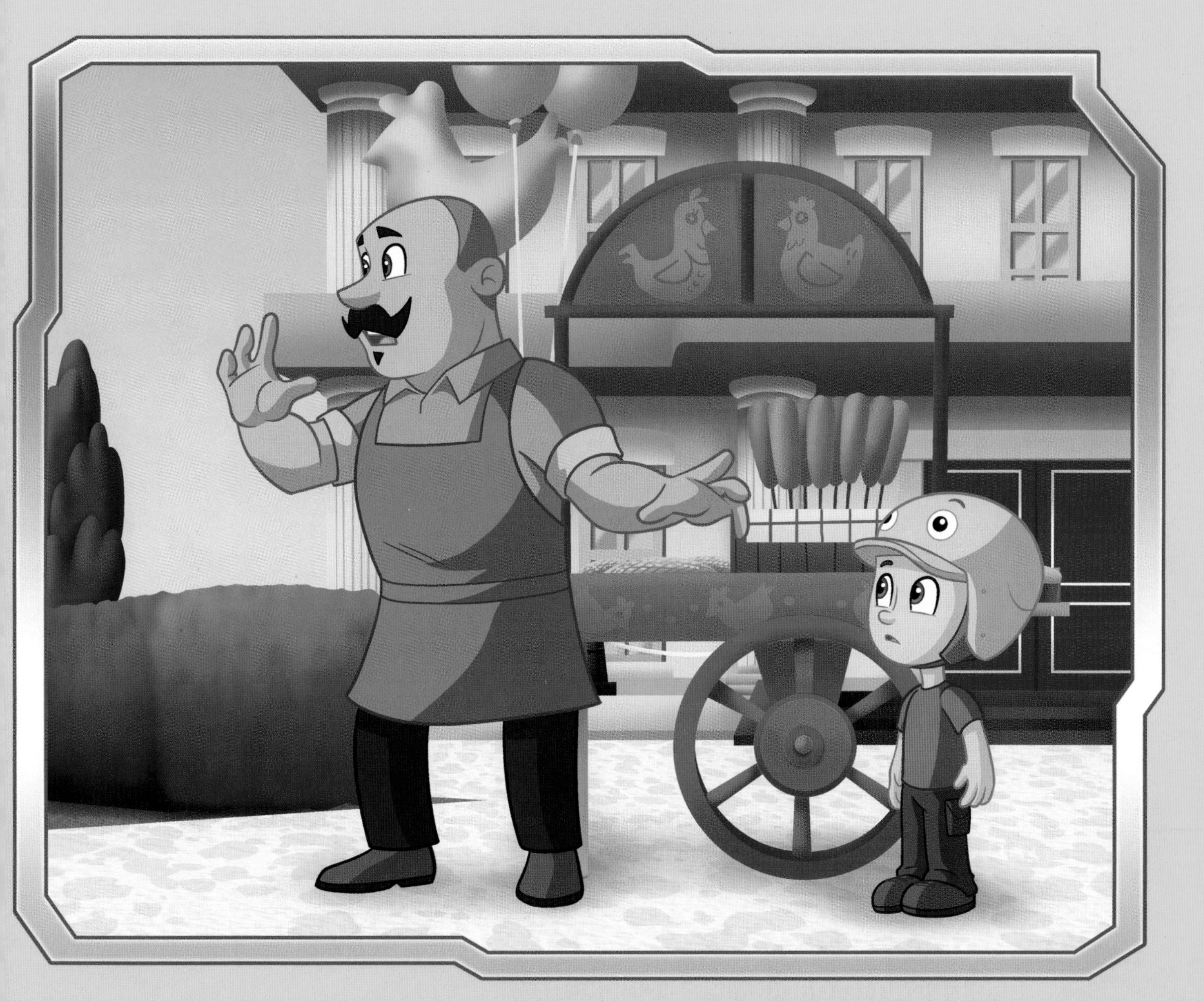

Meanwhile, at the Lookout, the PAW Patrol pups were practicing their dances for the party. DJ Rubble provided the music!

"Okay, Chase," said DJ Rubble. "This is your jam!"

"All right," said Chase. "Check out my Chickaletta *cha-cha*!" Chase began to dance like a chicken.

“Nice moves!” said Marshall.

“Yeah! Go, Chase!” said Zuma.

“Mayor Goodway and Chickaletta will be so surprised when we do a Chicken Day dance!” said Skye.

The pups howled as Marshall flew into the air. But almost as soon as he started his dance, Marshall fell on his face.

"Maybe I should call it the chicken *flop,*" he joked.

Back in town, Farmer Al arrived at city hall with a truck full of chicken feed.

Mayor Goodway smiled. "What a wonderfully appropriate way to celebrate Chicken Day."

"On the farm," said Farmer Al, "every day is Chicken Day . . . and Cow Day . . . and Sheep Day, too."

Farmer Al put a bag of chicken feed in the back of his truck, and Chickaletta couldn't resist it. The precious purse pet popped right on top of the bag and began eating from it. When Farmer Al drove off a few seconds later, he accidentally took the chicken with him!

Mayor Goodway soon noticed that Chickaletta was missing. "Where did she go? *Why* did she go? She's the chicken of honor!"

The mayor searched everywhere for Chickaletta. She was in such a panic, she didn't see Alex's skateboard until she stepped onto it and rolled away.

"Whoa!" she exclaimed. "How do I stop this thing?"

Mayor Goodway crashed into the statue of Chickaletta, and her costume got caught. She quickly called the PAW Patrol.

"Ryder!" she said. "I'm stuck in a chicken costume dangling from Chickaletta's statue on Chicken Day!"

"Oh, no!" said Ryder.

"But more important, Chickaletta is missing!" said the mayor.

"Don't worry, Mayor Goodway," said Ryder. "We're on our way! No job is too big, no chicken is too small!"

"PAW Patrol is on the roll!" said Ryder.

"Ryder! Oh, thank goodness you're here!" said Mayor Goodway. "The chicken of honor is missing!"

"We'll find her," said Ryder. "But let's get you down first."

Rocky used his mechanical claw to lift the mayor off the statue and put her down safely.

"Chickaletta has small, delicate feet," said Mayor Goodway. "She couldn't have gotten far."

"Spy Chase," said Ryder, "see if you can find her with your goggles."

With his heat-seeking goggles, Chase could see behind a bush—where some gophers were eating from Mr. Porter's missing popcorn machine!

"You found my popper!" said Mr. Porter.

"What's this?" asked Ryder. "Chicken feed?"

"Corn kernels? Chickens love 'em!" said Chase.

"Hmm, the corn kernels lead to those tire tracks," said Ryder.

"And Farmer Al brought some feed just this morning," added Mr. Porter.

Ryder told Skye to use her helicopter to see if she could find Chickaletta.

Hovering above Farmer Yumi's Farm, Skye spotted Farmer Al's truck . . . and Chickaletta!

"Great job, Skye," said Ryder. "We're on our way!"

Mayor Goodway, Ryder, and the pups soon reached Farmer Yumi's Farm.

Chickaletta ran to the mayor, then accidentally tripped and landed in a bucket. The bucket rolled across the farm and down the hill, and stopped in . . .

. . . a thorny thicket!

A wing on Mayor Goodway's costume got caught.

"Those thorns are pretty strong," said Ryder. "I'll help you out."

"Phew! Will we ever get Chickaletta out of this thorny mess?" asked the mayor.

"Yes, we will!" said Ryder.

Just then, a zip-line launcher emerged from Chase's backpack. It fired cables into the trees on either side of the thornbush. Chase slid along the line and rescued Chickaletta.

"Oh, Chickaletta, I thought I'd lost you!" said Mayor Goodway. "Then I found you . . . then nearly lost you again. We've certainly had enough excitement for one day, haven't we, my pet?"

She gave Chickaletta a big hug.

"Well, thank you, thank you, thank you, PAW Patrol!" said Mayor Goodway.

"You're welcome," said Ryder. "Whenever you have a problem, just cluck for help!"

"Now that you're safe and sound," the mayor said to Chickaletta, "Chicken Day can officially begin."

When they arrived at the park, they saw that DJ Rubble was rocking the party, playing great music that had everybody dancing.

"Look at the chicken of honor getting in the groove!" said Mayor Goodway, watching Chickaletta dance with her friends. "Oh, Chickaletta! Go, Chickie! Go, Chickie!"

ICE TEAM

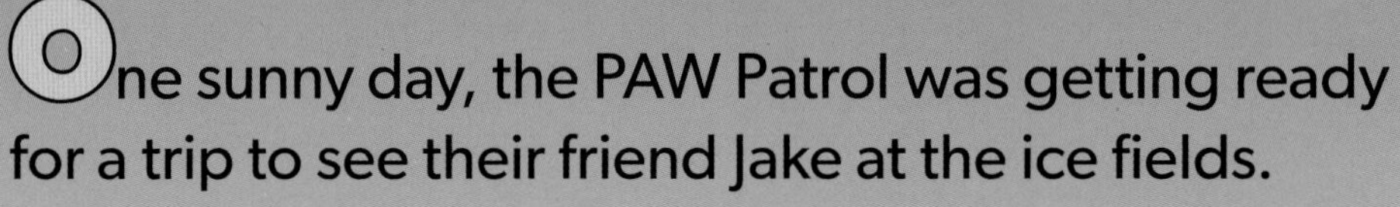

One sunny day, the PAW Patrol was getting ready for a trip to see their friend Jake at the ice fields.

Suddenly, there was a loud roar, and a big truck rolled up.

"Presenting the PAW Patroller!" Ryder announced. "It's a Lookout on wheels. It can take us anywhere!"

A door opened in the side and a mechanical dog hopped out.

"Robo Dog will be our driver!"

As Ryder was showing the pups around the PAW Patroller, Jake called.

"Hey, Jake! How are the ice fields?" Ryder asked.

"Amazing!" Jake declared. "Take a look!" The screen showed snowy hills and an icy river.

Just then, Jake slipped on the ice, and the pups could hear him yell, "My phone! My maps! All my stuff!"

Jake's equipment had splashed into the icy river!

"Jake's in big trouble!" Rubble exclaimed.

"Pups, get your vehicles," Ryder said.

The PAW Patroller's back door opened and a ramp came out. The pups quickly drove their vehicles aboard. Robo Dog started the engine and the PAW Patroller rolled into action.

At the ice fields, Jake was trying to get his backpack out of the water. But the riverbank was so icy that he began to slide in! Luckily, a husky pup pulled him out.

"Sweet save!" Jake said, then introduced himself.

"My name's Everest!" the pup exclaimed. "I rescued someone! I've always wanted to do a real rescue."

"We should probably get going," Everest said. "A storm's rolling in. I wouldn't want to lose my first real rescue in a blizzard. We can wait it out in my igloo. To get there, we can do this. . . ."

Everest flopped onto her belly and slid down the hill.

"Belly-bogganing!" Jake shouted, taking off after her. "Look out below!"

The two new friends slid along on the ice, zooming past some penguins.

When the PAW Patroller reached the ice fields, the snow was falling hard. The team started to look for Jake. They quickly found his frozen phone and pack.

"This means Jake doesn't have any supplies," Ryder said. Then he noticed something in the snow. "Are those tracks?"

Chase gave the tracks a sniff. "That's Jake, all right! And he's got another pup with him."

"Those tracks should lead us to Jake," Ryder announced. "Let's follow them."

As Chase followed the tracks on the ground, Skye took to the frosty air. "This pup's got to fly!"

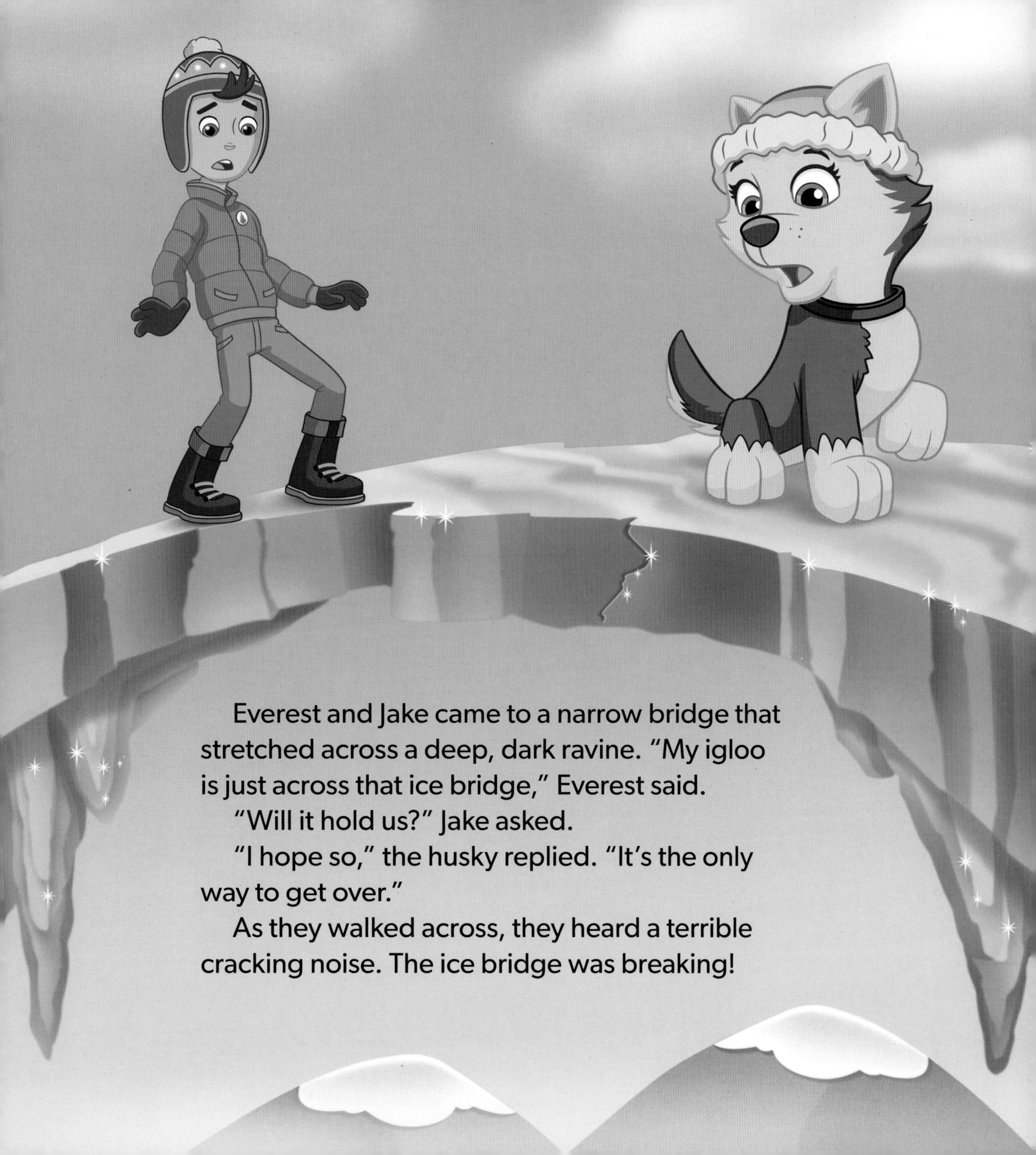

Everest and Jake came to a narrow bridge that stretched across a deep, dark ravine. “My igloo is just across that ice bridge,” Everest said.

“Will it hold us?” Jake asked.

“I hope so,” the husky replied. “It’s the only way to get over.”

As they walked across, they heard a terrible cracking noise. The ice bridge was breaking!

Just as the bridge collapsed, Skye swooped in, catching Jake and Everest with a rope. But before she had carried them to the other side of the ravine, the rope broke.

"Jump!" Jake yelled.

Everest landed on a ledge, but Jake missed it. He caught the edge with his fingers and dangled over the dark ravine.

"Don't worry!" Everest yelled. "I've got you!" She snagged Jake's sleeve and pulled him to safety. "Yes—two rescues in one day!"

Everyone went to Jake's cabin on the mountain for roasted marshmallows—and a surprise.

"Everest," Jake said, "I could use a smart pup like you to help out on the mountain."

"And for saving Jake and showing great rescue skills," Ryder added, "I'd like to make you an official member of the PAW Patrol!"

"This is the best day ever!" Everest exclaimed, and all the pups cheered.

PUP-
FU
POWER!

It was a special day for Farmer Yumi's martial arts students. The PAW Patrol, Mayor Goodway, and Chickaletta were all gathered in her barn, eager to earn their Pup-Fu yellow belts.

"Students, are you ready?" asked Farmer Yumi. The pups lined up and bowed to their sensei.

One by one, the pups showed off their moves. Rocky twirled a staff, and Marshall spun. Skye kicked high, and Rubble stood tall. Zuma was ready for action. Chase announced, "And now I will—ah . . . ah . . . *CHOO!* I'm sorry. I'm a little allergic to . . . *kittens?*"

It was the Kitten Catastrophe Crew from Foggy Bottom! They had snuck into Farmer Yumi's barn.

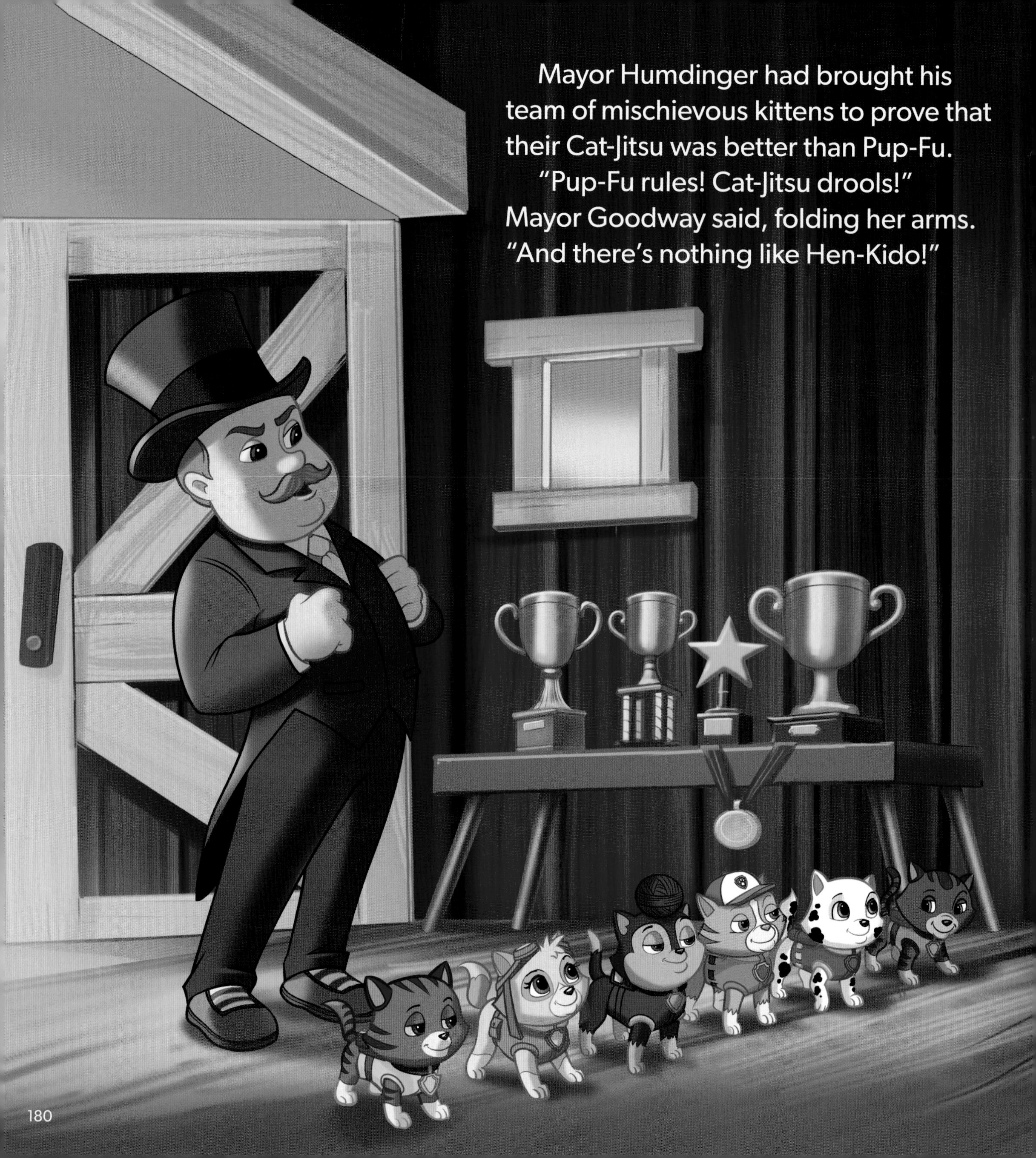

Mayor Humdinger had brought his team of mischievous kittens to prove that their Cat-Jitsu was better than Pup-Fu.

"Pup-Fu rules! Cat-Jitsu drools!" Mayor Goodway said, folding her arms. "And there's nothing like Hen-Kido!"

"Bwok!" Chickaletta clucked in agreement and gave a quick kick.

"It's not about which art is superior," Farmer Yumi said. "The point is for all pups, kittens, mayors, and chickens to do their best."

Mayor Humdinger clapped his hands, and his Kitten Catastrophe Crew sprang into action. They jumped and kicked and rolled on balls. One kitten headed for the zip line.

"I'll show you how a Pup-Fu master uses the zip line," Marshall said as he jumped up and grabbed the cord. *"Wheeee!"*

A mechanical claw belonging to one mischievous kitten popped out of his pack and hooked on to the line.

Ziiing! Marshall went flying!

Marshall crashed to the ground.

"Are you okay?" Rubble asked.

"Sure," Marshall replied. "A Pup-Fu master always knows exactly how to land when they fall."

"For the next part of our belt test, we will have sparring," Farmer Yumi said.

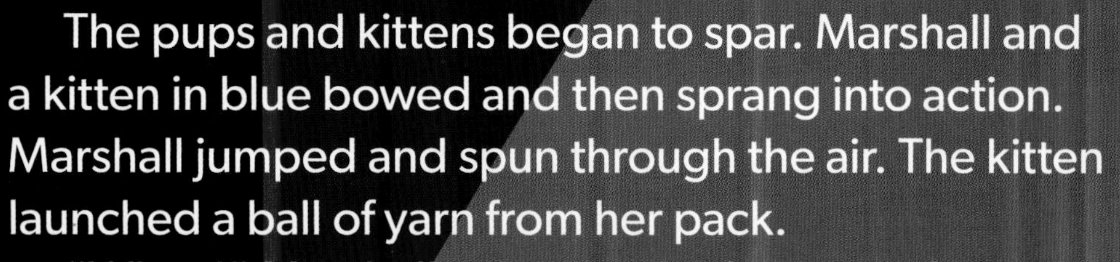

The pups and kittens began to spar. Marshall and a kitten in blue bowed and then sprang into action. Marshall jumped and spun through the air. The kitten launched a ball of yarn from her pack.

"Whoa!" Marshall yelped as he fell to the floor. His legs were wrapped in yarn.

"Pup-Fu?" Mayor Humdinger snickered. "That looks like pup fail!"

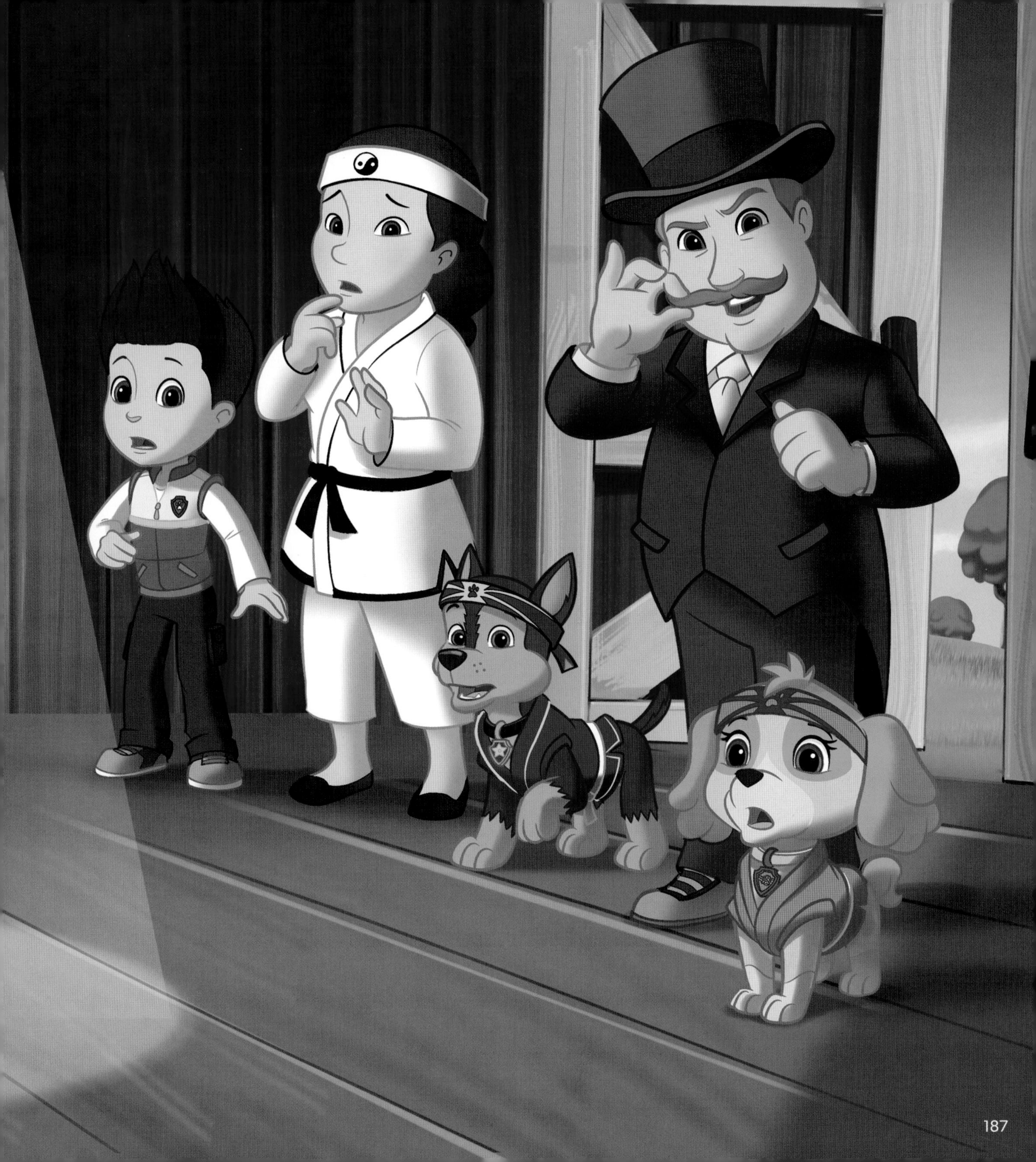

It was time to award the belts. Farmer Yumi gave each pup a golden yellow belt. She was proud of them and their dedication to Pup-Fu. "Your extra-hard work would please the ancient masters."

But there were no belts for the kittens.

"Mayor Humdinger," Farmer Yumi said, "until your kittens learn to control themselves and their tools, I'm afraid they cannot earn their yellow belts."

“Hooray for the PAW Patrol!” Ryder cheered. They were all good pups—and they were all very good sports.

PIT
CREW
PUPS

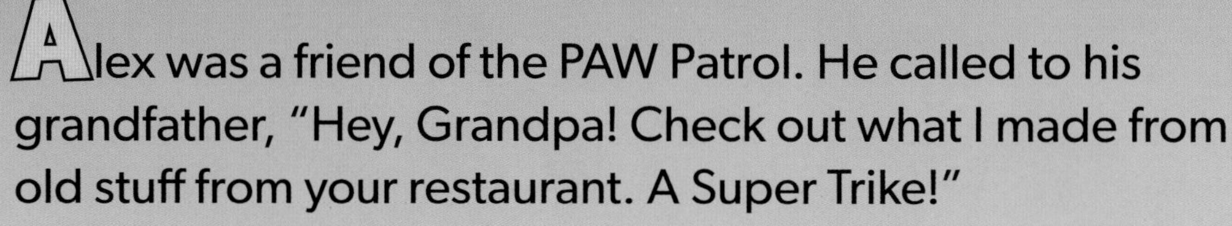

Alex was a friend of the PAW Patrol. He called to his grandfather, "Hey, Grandpa! Check out what I made from old stuff from your restaurant. A Super Trike!"

"Very nice!" Grandpa said.

"Look," Alex said. "I made a brake out of a pizza paddle!"

"And you used lots of duct tape!" Grandpa said.

"Just like you taught me," Alex said.

"Watch this, Grandpa!" Alex said. "I'm going to go super fast on my Super Trike!"

First he tightened his helmet. Then he grabbed the handlebars, ran as fast as he could, jumped in, and pedaled hard.

"*Whoo-hoo!*" he cried as he raced down the sidewalk.

But the Super Trike hit a little bump and flew into the air. *WHUMP!* When the bike landed, it fell apart.

"My Super Trike!" Alex wailed.

Parts flew everywhere. Some even rolled into the street.

"Now I have to put it all back together again," Alex said sadly.

"I know who can help you!" Grandpa said.

Grandpa called Ryder.

"Hello?" Ryder said. "Ryder here."

"Hi, Ryder," Grandpa said. "I have a bit of an emergency."

He explained what happened to Alex's bike. "I know you're pretty handy with gadgets and vehicles."

"Tell him we're on our way!" Ryder said. "No job is too big, no pup is too small!"

Ryder called the PAW Patrol. They jumped into their vehicles and zoomed across the bridge to town. *VROOOOM!*

Ryder led the way on his four-wheeler. Chase drove his customized squad car. Rocky followed in his repair truck. And Skye flew overhead in her helicopter!

“Let’s secure the work zone,” Chase said. In the street, he put orange cones around the scattered parts of Alex’s Super Trike.

Next he spoke to the drivers through his megaphone. “Please find an alternate route. PAW Patrol at work!”

The cars turned around and drove down a different street.

Ryder and Alex picked up the parts.

“Can you fix it?” Alex asked.

“Sure we can!” Ryder said.

Back at the Lookout, Ryder, Rocky, and Chase put the Super Trike back together. They also added some new parts. And instead of duct tape, they used screws and rivets to fasten the parts together.

"These will hold better," Rocky said.

"But my grandpa fixes *everything* with duct tape," Alex said.

"I think it's done!" Ryder announced.

"Awesome!" Alex shouted. "Now my Super Trike can go super fast! C'mon, Ryder! Let's race!"

"First we need to test it, and then you need to get used to it," Ryder said. "Try riding it slowly."

But Alex didn't want to go slowly. He jumped on his Super Trike and took off, pedaling as hard as he could.

"Alex, wait!" Ryder called. "You're going too fast!"

Alex zoomed down a hill. "Wow, this is fast!"

But it was *too* fast. Alex took his feet off the pedals.

Ryder rode up behind him. "Slow down! Use the brakes!"

"I can't get my feet back on the pedals!" Alex cried. "They're turning too fast!"

Ryder looked ahead and saw that Alex was racing right toward a busy street!

"Chase!" Ryder yelled. "Secure the traffic!"

"Chase is on the case!" he called. He took a shortcut down a hill with his lights flashing and his siren blaring. He pulled into traffic.

"Please stop!" he said to the drivers. "PAW Patrol emergency in progress!" All the cars stopped.

Just then, Alex and Ryder zipped by onto the bridge.

Ryder called Skye. “I need you and your copter at the bridge!”

“Let’s take to the sky!” she said.

Skye flew straight to the bridge. Then she lowered a hook to catch the back of Alex’s trike to slow him down.

She missed it twice, but on her third try, she did it! “Got him!” she said.

The trike stopped. Alex got off and waved up to Skye. "Yay, Skye! Great flying!"

"That *was* some pretty good flying," Ryder agreed.

"Aw," Skye said modestly. "It was no biggie."

"Are you all right, Alex?" Ryder asked.

"I'm okay," he said. "I just couldn't stop it. My Super Trike is *too* super!"

The pups joined Ryder and Alex on the bridge.

"I'm sorry, Ryder," Alex said. "This is all my fault. If I had slowed down like you said, this wouldn't have happened."

"That's okay, Alex," Ryder said. "But whenever you try something new, you have to start out easy."

Alex nodded and smiled. "I know. I just wanted to be like you, Ryder!"

"You were such good pups today, how about we head to the lemonade stand?" Ryder suggested.

"Yeah!" Alex cheered, ringing the bell on his Super Trike. "Let's race on over!"

Skye cleared her throat, and Chase shook his head.

"I mean *roll* on over," Alex said.

They all got into their vehicles and rode to the lemonade stand safely.

"Good work, Alex!" Ryder said. "You've earned the PAW Patrol Safe Driving Cup."

He handed Alex a trophy.

"Wowie!" Alex said. "Thanks, Ryder!"

"You've also won a spoon," Ryder added.

Alex looked confused. "A spoon? Why?"

Ryder took the top off the trophy. It was full of ice cream! "'Cause it's an *ice cream* cup!"

"Yay!" Alex cheered.

Chase's
Space
Case

One starry night, Ryder, Skye, and Rocky were gazing up at the sky.

"A star is falling!" Skye said.

Ryder checked with his binoculars. "Hmm that doesn't look like a star to me," he said. "It seems to be some kind of spaceship!"

"Cool!" Rocky and Skye said.

"And it's headed for Adventure Bay!" Ryder said.

CRASH! The spaceship slammed into Farmer Yumi's barn!

Strange glowing rings came out of the spaceship, and they formed a big green bubble around Farmer Yumi's cow, Bettina.

The bubble lifted Bettina into the air! *MOOOOO!*

Mayor Goodway was at a square dance in Farmer Yumi's barn. When she came out of the barn, she saw Bettina trapped in the floating bubble!

She called Ryder right away. "Can you help poor Bettina and find out what's going on here?"

"We're on it, Mayor Goodway," Ryder promised. "No job is too big, no pup is too small!"

Ryder called the other members of the PAW Patrol and told them about Bettina's problem.

They jumped into their vehicles and raced to Farmer Yumi's barn. The shining stars lit their way.

"PAW Patrol is on the roll!" Ryder shouted.

When they reached the barn, they saw Bettina still floating in the bubble.

"Weird," Chase said. "How does she stay up there?"

"I don't know," Ryder said. "But I think *this* might have something to do with it!" He pointed at the crashed spaceship.

With the suction cups from Chase's zip line, the pups pulled Bettina out of the green bubble.

"Chase, I need you to use your spy gear to find the pilot of that spaceship," Ryder said.

"Yes, sir, Ryder, sir!" Chase said. "Night-vision goggles!" Green goggles slid down from Chase's helmet to cover his eyes and help him see in the dark. He sniffed the ground, searching for the missing pilot.

Chase didn't find the pilot—he found Mayor Goodway and Chickaletta trapped in a floating bubble!

"How did you two get up there?" he cried.

"A little green space alien beamed us up!" Mayor Goodway explained.

Chase used the net in his backpack to pull the mayor and Chickaletta out of the green bubble. Then he continued his search for the little green space alien.

Chase found something. "A round green head!" He looked closer. "Oops. It's just a melon."

He looked around and saw that he was in a field of melons. He walked down one row. "Melon . . . melon . . . space alien . . . melon . . . Wait—*space alien*?"

The little alien looked scared. *"Baw! Buh-bee! Buh-baw-baw-baw!"* he said.

"Sorry," said Chase, "but I don't understand what you're saying!"

The alien pointed at Chase, and yellow rings came out of his finger. A green bubble formed around the pup and lifted him up!

"Whoa!" Chase yelped.

The little green alien ran off, leaving Chase trapped in the floating bubble!

Chase tried to push his way out of the bubble, but he was stuck. "Help! Help! Anybody?" he called.

He got an idea. "If I can pull Bettina and the mayor free, I can pull myself out, too! Zip line!"

The zip line shot out of his backpack and attached itself to two trees. Chase slid down the line and out of the bubble!

The alien made his way to the Lookout—which looked like a spaceship to him!

Ryder and the pups found the alien trying to fly the Lookout. He wanted to go home to his mom.

Ryder pulled out his PupPad and made a call. "Rocky, how's it going with fixing that spaceship? Are you close?"

"Yes!" Rocky said. "Look out the window!"

Ryder, the pups, and the alien all ran to the window and saw Rocky flying the spaceship! He had fixed it with some old parts he'd found in his truck. A pink coat hanger made a fine antenna. A bicycle wheel worked as part of the landing gear.

"Don't lose it—reuse it!" Rocky said.

The alien hopped up and down happily. *"Bay-bay-bay-bay! Buh-bah-buh-bah!"*

Ryder kneeled and said to the alien, "Whenever you're in trouble, just yelp—or *beep-beep-beep*—for help! C'mon!" He led the way into the spaceship.

The happy little alien flew his new spaceship with Rocky and Ryder in it. Then he beamed the rest of the PAW Patrol aboard.

"We're flying in a spaceship!" Skye said. "Sweet!"

"Awesome!" the others agreed.

As they flew over Adventure Bay, they waved to Mayor Goodway and Chickaletta.

"Coolest ride ever!" Ryder said.

The little green alien beamed the pups and Ryder onto the field in front of the Lookout.

As the alien flew back to his home planet and his family, Ryder and the PAW Patrol waved goodbye to their new friend.

PUP, PUP, AND AWAY!

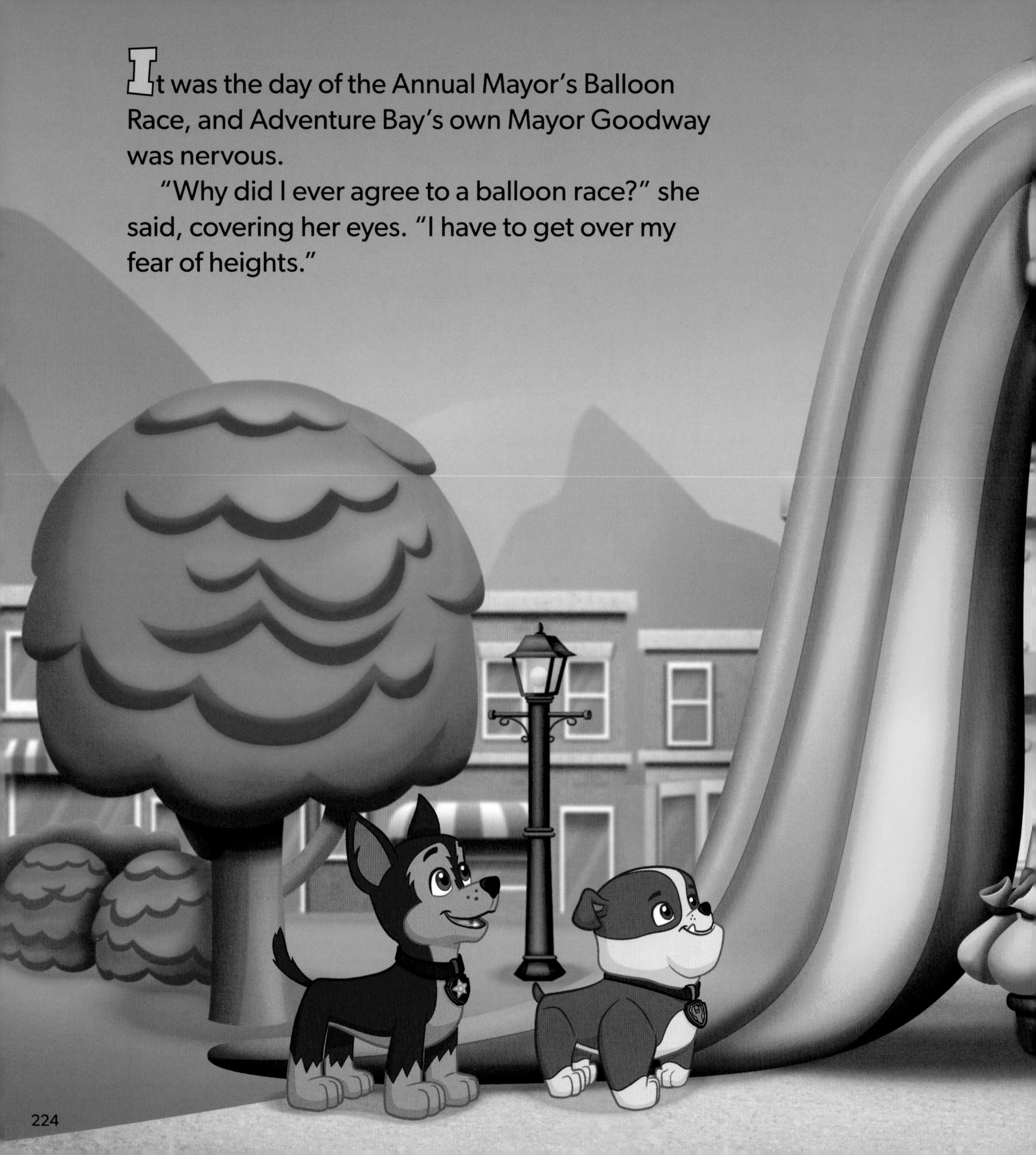

It was the day of the Annual Mayor's Balloon Race, and Adventure Bay's own Mayor Goodway was nervous.

"Why did I ever agree to a balloon race?" she said, covering her eyes. "I have to get over my fear of heights."

"Don't worry. I'll be in the balloon to help you," said Ryder. "Ready to unroll the balloon, pups?"

"We're ready!" Rubble barked.

Rubble and Chase unrolled the dusty balloon.

"Uh-oh!" Chase said. "It's got a . . . a . . . *ACHOO!*" When he had stopped sneezing from the dust, he continued, ". . . a hole! A ripped balloon can't hold air!"

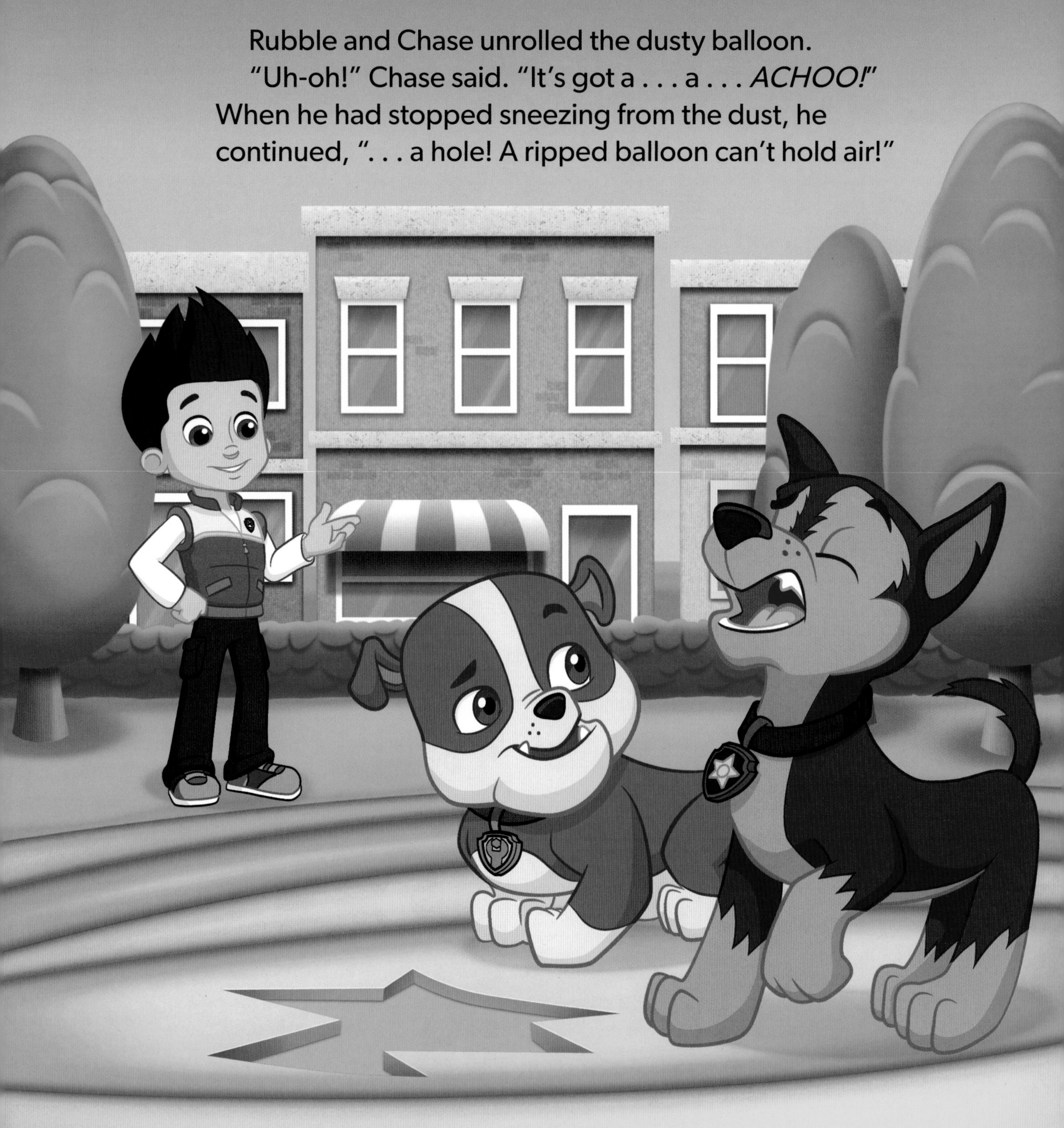

Mayor Goodway groaned. "Mayor Humdinger from Foggy Bottom will win again!"

"Don't worry," Ryder said. "We'll get this balloon ready for the race. No job is too big, no pup is too small."

Ryder pulled out his PupPad and called the rest of the PAW Patrol.

The PAW Patrol quickly assembled at the Lookout. "Ready for action, Ryder, sir!" Chase barked.

Ryder told the pups about the mayor's balloon. "We need to fix the balloon for the race. Rocky, can you find something in your recycling truck that we can use to patch it?"

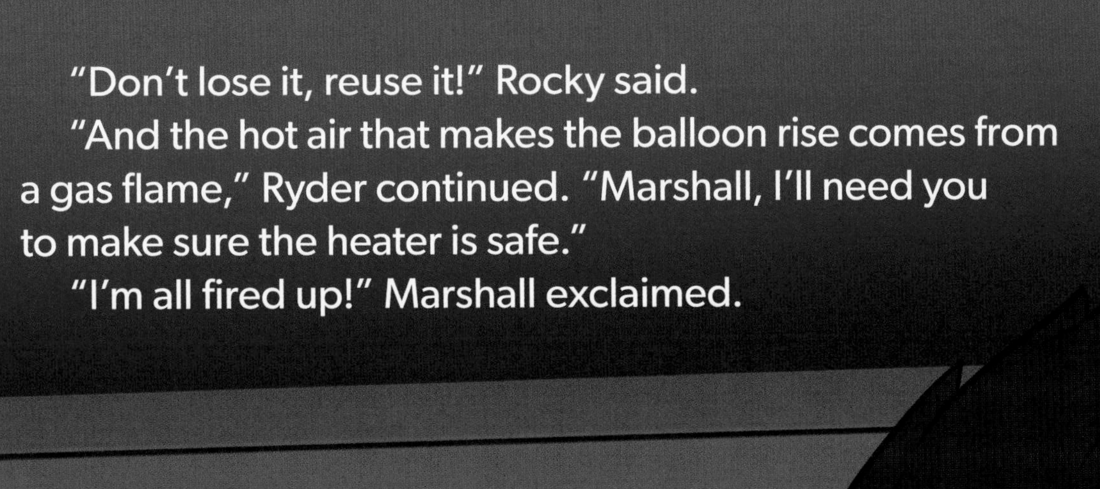

"Don't lose it, reuse it!" Rocky said.

"And the hot air that makes the balloon rise comes from a gas flame," Ryder continued. "Marshall, I'll need you to make sure the heater is safe."

"I'm all fired up!" Marshall exclaimed.

The PAW Patrol raced to the town square. Rocky quickly inspected the tear in the balloon. "I've got the perfect patch in my truck," he said.

"And how do the gas tanks look?" Ryder asked.

"The big question is how do they smell," Marshall replied. He sniffed the tanks. "I don't smell any gas leaks."

Rocky glued a piece of Zuma's old surf kite over the hole.

"Good work!" Ryder exclaimed. "That patch is a perfect fit."

Ryder turned a lever and the balloon slowly filled with hot air. The other balloons were gathering on the horizon. The race was about to begin.

"Time to get over my fear of heights!" the mayor shouted. "I'm going to win this race!"

She pumped her fist and accidentally hit the lever on the heater, flipping it all the way open. The balloon started to fly away!

Marshall chased after the balloon. He jumped and grabbed a rope with his teeth. But the balloon didn't stop. Instead, Marshall was pulled higher and higher into the air.

Suddenly, the rope slid from Marshall's mouth and he fell!

Marshall landed right in Ryder's arms. "Thanks, Ryder!" he barked.

The race had started, and there was no time to waste. Ryder called Skye on his PupPad.

"Mayor Goodway took off without me! I need you to fly me to her balloon in your copter."

Skye slid into her Pup House, which quickly turned into a helicopter. “Let’s take to the sky!” she exclaimed as she zoomed into the air.

Skye flew to Ryder and dropped a harness down to him. He locked himself in, and Skye whisked him away.

"I'll swing you over to the balloon," Skye said. But she had to hurry because the balloon was headed straight for the lighthouse on Seal Island!

Ryder sailed through the air, reached out, and caught the basket!

Mayor Goodway helped Ryder climb into the balloon. He quickly gave it a burst of hot air and it rose over the lighthouse.

"Made it, Skye," Ryder reported as he undid his harness.

"Roger that!" Skye said, flying away. "Go win that trophy!"

"All right, Mayor Goodway, are you ready to win this race?" The mayor gave Ryder a thumbs-up. "I'm in it to win it! They raced after the other balloons.

With Ryder at the controls, the balloon quickly caught up with Mayor Humdinger, who was in the lead.

"The race is on!" Ryder yelled.

"I've never lost a race, and I'm not starting now!" Mayor Humdinger shouted back.

With a rush of hot air, Ryder and Mayor Goodway's balloon whooshed past Mayor Humdinger.

"There's Jake's Mountain!" Mayor Goodway exclaimed. "The finish line is on the other side!"

"The winds are stronger up high," Ryder said.
"We'll have a better chance of winning if we go up."
"Up, up, and away!" Mayor Goodway cheered.

Ryder guided the balloon higher and rode the rushing winds over Jake's Mountain—but Mayor Humdinger did the same! His balloon zipped right past Ryder and Mayor Goodway.

Down on the ground, all the PAW Patrol pups cheered as the balloons came into view. Mayor Humdinger's balloon swooped out of the sky first . . . but Mayor Goodway and Ryder dropped ahead of him at the last second and crossed the finish line. They won the race!

Mayor Humdinger sadly handed the trophy to Mayor Goodway. "I believe this belongs to you."

Mayor Goodway gave the trophy to Ryder. "This belongs to Ryder and the PAW Patrol."

"Thanks, Mayor Goodway!" Ryder said with a smile. "Whenever you need a hand, just yelp for help!"